never

trust

a *happy*

song

Text © 2014 by Natalie Bina
Cover design by Natalie Bina

The characters and events portrayed in this book are fictitious, or have been worded to represent fictitious circumstances surrounding the characters. The thoughts, opinions, and actions of the characters are not meant to directly represent those of any real person, living or dead.

Stanford University does offer summer sessions for high school students. However, this book does not accurately depict the study experiences that Stanford offers.

Printed in the United States of America.
Title set in Georgia, text set in Times New Roman.

Printed by Createspace.com, a DBA of On-Demand Publishing, LLC

For Erin,

*who inspires me with her work ethic,
and frightens me with her ability to go without sleep.*

Thank you for being my borrowed sister.

"I mean, yes, we're sinking.
But the music is exceptional."

– said during the sinking
of the Titanic

chapter *1*

There's nothing worse than having to spend your summer in a town full of people you don't know. Or so I've been told, though my own experience with holidays and strangers provides no evidence to support such a hypothesis. Admittedly, my knowledge of carefree vacations and fun times with friends is rather scanty. Even the sixth graders I tutored seemed to have more experience with summer escapades than I did. As the end of the school year approached, they began to complain about the boring summer trips their families planned to subject them to.

Their voices echoed in my mind as I sprawled in the back of the minivan on the long drive to Palo Alto. Their faces had twisted with sympathy at the news that I would spend the summer with a family I had never met, and the sympathy had turned to horror when I explained that the purpose of the trip was to attend an academic program.

"School?" one of the sixth grade boys exclaimed. "You're going all the way to the Bay Area for *school*?"

I nodded and returned my gaze to the geometry lesson, where I was illustrating how all corresponding angles are equal when a transversal intersects two parallel lines, but the boy's voice intervened.

"I mean, it's almost *San Francisco*! You could spend your time at the beach or go to a theme park or go shopping or celebrity hunting or–"

"Separate the series, please," I interrupted casually, looking up at him from the practice worksheet I was preparing.

natalie bina

"What?"

"Separate the series. When listing items in a series you can't string them together with 'or'; you must use a comma. You should get into the habit of it now, because it's a skill you'll no doubt be tested on."

The boy just stared at me, blinking a few times before turning to his friend, who was also staring at me as if I had sprouted a second head.

The memory of their bewildered looks made me giggle, and I smiled into the mesh of my seatbelt. If I missed anything about home this summer, it would be the students I tutored during the school year.

"Cassidy." My mother's voice intruded from the front of the car, clipped and full of purpose. "Have you started your practice work? Remember that you need to finish that whole workbook that came in the mail." Mom was still facing forward, but as she said this she made eye contact with me through the rearview mirror, and the quick glimpse of her steely green eye was enough for me to imagine the expression on her face.

"Yes, Mom, I started working on the book as soon as it arrived. I'm on chapter four."

"*Four* –" Mom began, an edge sneaking into her already tense voice.

"Out of five," I interjected. "Four out of five chapters, Mom. Don't worry."

She would worry, though. No matter what I told her, no matter what I accomplished, Mom would inevitably worry, as if a momentary lapse in attention might send me hurtling off the cliff of academic achievement and plunging into the fiery abyss of future-damaging GPAs. Her fear was superfluous because, in reality, I was so far back from the cliff that I couldn't even *see* the edge.

"Well, all right then," she said, although she hesitated after the 'well' in a way that let me know something wasn't all right. "Are you sleeping now?"

"Trying to."

"Okay," she said, and I knew that was the end of the conversation. My mother's 'okay's were similar to periods. They brought everything to a full stop.

I wasn't tired, but I wanted a moment of respite from parental attention. I ducked under the shoulder strap of the seatbelt and flopped sideways on the seat, swiveling my head to stare up through the sunroof. From that position I watched tree after dusty tree zoom by on the mountainside, much like the precalculus formulas parading through my head. It was impossible to stop the flow of information, even as I tried to rest. We passed a tree that was bent over like the top of the number 2, and that immediately made me think of the double angle formula. $\sin 2x = 2 \sin x \cos x$, I thought. *Don't forget it, Cassidy. Think of a tree, branching off into two different limbs, one called sine and one called cosine.*

The repetitive movement of the trees zooming by was soothing, and I switched to wondering whether I would actually like Palo Alto and Stanford. During freshman year, my mother had decided that I should go away for the summers to study. Now, going away for the second time, the process was starting to feel like a comfortable routine. Mom signs me up for a program, I get my practice work, Mom drives me to the location, she drops me off, and I start school. It was a simple sequence. If I had a choice, I would keep it that way, with no changes. But I already knew that this year would be different.

"Cassidy," my mother said, even though she had told me to go to sleep, "unlike last summer, you are going to be near a big city. There will be more distractions – museums, concerts, restaurants, plus all the tourist traps of San Francisco. I want you to promise me that you won't get distracted."

"Yes, Mom," I replied in a monotone.

"And no matter how much your host family tries to drag you out on excursions, remember your priorities."

"Yes, Mom." I buried my face in the upholstery at the unpleasant reminder that I would be staying with a host family. No quiet dorm room with a quiet roommate who was doing the exact same things that I was. No easy access to the library and the classrooms. I would have to commute to campus every day, and – when not at Stanford – somehow socialize with my host family.

"What are their names?" I asked.

"Whose?"

"My host family's. Do you know what their names are?"

"No," she replied. "All it said on the form was that their last name was Harper."

Harper. Something about that name reminded me of the classic families of the 50s. I conjured up the pictures from my favorite history textbook's chapter on 1950s family economy. *The standard structure of an American family in the 1950s: a working father, a mother who stayed at home and looked after the children, and two children.* The mom probably liked to cook, and the kids probably had a dog that barked whenever people came to the door. I wondered what kind of school the Harper kids went to. I knew it was probably nothing like mine, and I could already make an educated guess that relating to this mysterious family was going to be difficult.

After that thought, sleep did come. As I dozed off, I was vaguely aware that I was in a very uncomfortable position, one where I would wake up with an imprint of the seatbelt on my cheek.

"Cassidy, did you fall asleep on your textbook again?" Mom asked after some time, when I must have groggily sat up. Her words woke me from my half-sleep.

"Huh? Uh, no, I'm ... I'm not sure ...." Mom waved her hand, no doubt realizing that my confused state was not going to produce the rational response she wanted.

"Well, we're here," she said. I bolted fully upright and realized that the car was no longer moving. My unconscious state must have kept me from noticing our deceleration, which was odd, because usually I was quite in sync with Newton's Laws.

"Where is here?" I asked, the words coming slowly. The scenery had changed from the jagged rocks of the mountains to a flat and lavish neighborhood, complete with large estates in pastel colors.

"Your home for the next three months. Look around." I did as I was told, and taking in the house before me, I knew for sure that this family would be different.

The house was huge and immaculately groomed. I could imagine English royalty living there if they had resided in modern California. I stepped out of the car and onto a soft lawn, greener than any I'd seen before, and immediately felt small.

"Mom, this place is enormous," I said as I turned to her. "Tell me again why I'm staying here instead of the dorms."

My mother rolled her eyes, visibly miffed. "I've already told you, the program requires every student to stay with a host family. Families who live nearby volunteer, and then a student is assigned to them." She paused to do a onceover of the house. "Their house looks very nice. You should feel lucky that you were assigned to them."

"I have nothing against them," I muttered. "I just …." But I didn't complete my sentence, not wanting to give Mom another reason to harp on about the dangers of getting distracted.

"There's no need to decide already about whether you'll like it here," she said, walking over to rub my shoulders. "You haven't even met them yet."

"Well, there's a remedy for that." I disconnected myself from my mother's hands and marched up to the door. I pressed down hard on the doorbell button, to show this family that I had purpose.

A tall woman answered the door, and I knew that she must be the mother. Her hair was shoulder length and brown, and I smelled sugar wafting from her skin. *Definitely a baker.*

"Hello," I said crisply. "I'm–"

"You must be Cassidy!" she cried, pulling me into a hug. Her immense height and my petite frame did not mesh well geometrically, making the hug uncomfortable.

"Yes," I responded as clearly as possible in my current position. "And you must be Mrs. Harper."

"Call me Mallory," she said, smiling widely. Everything about the woman seemed magnified. Just her presence was enough to make me feel like I was being pushed downwards. And, as nice as her offer was, I wasn't sure I'd ever be comfortable with calling her by her first name.

"I'm Meredith," my mom said, her voice brusque in comparison, "Cassidy's mother."

"Oh, so nice to meet you!" Mrs. Harper sang. "Please, come in."

If the outside of the Harpers' house was lavish, then the inside was even more so. My attention was first drawn to the intricate carpets on the floor, and the shiny wood areas that were not covered. *Lots of light, exaggerated designs, and pastel colors.* The designs looked like those of the Baroque style that I'd seen in an art history textbook. *Part classic family of the 1950s, part English royalty,* I thought. *What an irrational mix.*

As I took in every detail of the house, I heard Mrs. Harper introduce my mother to Mr. Harper, and my mother compliment them on the state of their lawn. Their voices became fuzzy as I stared up at the huge glass chandelier above me. Each piece of glass curved smoothly outwards, creating a spider-like shape. It looked as though at any moment it could fall and impale me with its shards.

I followed the tour into what I guessed to be the dining room, where a large table sat covered with plates of food.

"Oh, please don't let us interrupt your dinner," Mom said as soon as she saw the table.

"No, no, this is for you!" Mrs. Harper replied, guiding my mom towards one of the chairs.

"For us?" my mom repeated, even though she had obviously heard Mrs. Harper loud and clear. "No really, that's quite all right. I really should help Cassidy get settled and then be going, as it's quite a long drive back."

"Exactly!" Mrs. Harper exclaimed, her words beginning less than a second after my mom had finished hers. "We wanted a chance to spend some time together with you and Cassidy before you take off."

Mom began to fidget, and her hand crept up to grip the back of one of the chairs – a crack in her normally purposeful mannerisms. "Really, there's no need. You're already taking on the task of housing my daughter for the summer, and–"

"Oh, don't be silly!" Mrs. Harper exclaimed, cutting her off. "It's going to be great having her here. We all agree that this is going to be fun."

I cringed. I did consider parts of the summer school process to be fun, but I was certain that my definition of fun was very different from theirs. I assumed that Mom would lecture Mrs. Harper on the seriousness of my situation, but instead she just gave her a tight smile. "Well, all right. Why not?" my mom said as she looked at me, and I got the feeling that I was supposed to answer the question.

I frowned, wondering why Mom had backed down. It seemed better to me that everyone get on the same page sooner rather than later. And the Harpers seemed to be in a completely different book, one where meals were social occasions and there was time for small conversation.

Then, a man I assumed to be Mr. Harper made his way into my line of sight. He was tall and lean, and I imagined him morphing into a cat and curling his skinny body up to a warm fire. "I don't believe I've introduced myself," he said, walking up to me. "I'm Don."

"Hi, Mr. Harper," I replied. "I'm Cassidy."

Mr. Harper chuckled, "I know." Then he tilted his head and gave his wife a look. "Should we call Grace?"

"Oh, yes," she responded. "I'll go get her."

Silence fell after Mrs. Harper left the room. I soon grew uncomfortable, and my eyes wandered away from the scene at hand. I noticed the incredible detail surrounding the entrance where Mr. Harper had emerged. The doorway was wide, and could be closed by pulling in two enormous wood-framed panels of glass. The doorway was lined with embellished wood that eventually transitioned into the rosy color of the walls. The curvy embossing reminded me of the RNA patterns that I'd been studying on the drive up. Then my eyes landed on Grace Harper.

"I'm guessing she's your daughter," I said, gesturing to the girl who had appeared in the doorway. "She certainly has the same tall-and-skinny gene."

As she squeezed past the girl, Mrs. Harper's laugh echoed around the room. "Yes, this is Grace." She turned and motioned the girl forward. "Come introduce yourself."

Grace's slender frame was dominated by a pair of baggy overalls that hid most of a brightly tie-dyed t-shirt. My knowledge of pop culture was lacking, but I suspected that the fist-pumping logo on the t-shirt represented a superhero. As Grace bounced across the room toward us, her shoulder-length hair seemed to defy the laws of gravity as it flew up into the air.

The next thing I registered was that I was being hugged. I tried not to squirm. "Hi!" Grace exclaimed after she pulled back. "You must be Cassidy."

"Yes," I replied slowly.

"Well, I'm Grace," she said, placing her hand on her heart.

"I know."

Grace giggled, and it sounded like the higher-pitched twin of her mother's laugh. At that moment, Hrs. Harper succeeded in getting my mother to sit down at the table, and Mr. Harper, who I hadn't noticed leaving, came back into the room with even more plates of food.

I realized then that this family was actually really nice. They were all well-meaning, pleasant people, and I guessed that they were just trying to be polite. But as I sat down across from my mother and caught her gaze, I saw that she felt as uncomfortable as I did. For now I still had her companionship, but she would soon leave, and I would have no one but the Harpers. No one but the overwhelmingly tall, skinny, giggly, big-house Harpers. And though they were nice, they weren't Mom, and I wasn't sure they understood me.

There's nothing worse than having to spend your summer in a town full of people you don't know. I wondered if the unpleasant feeling growing in my stomach was what my sixth graders had meant by that.

chapter 2

As Mom said goodbye, I felt like a soldier being sent off to the front lines in World War I. She hugged me harder than she ever had before, then cupped my face in her hands.

"Good luck," she said very seriously, and I knew that message extended to multiple matters.

"Thanks," I replied. "You don't have to worry. I'll work hard."

Mom didn't reply, but hugged me again, and tighter. My front was so smashed into hers that for a second I worried that her grip might rupture my spleen. Then I wondered if this meant she was going to miss me.

"Remember, I'll be visiting in July," she said after relinquishing her hold.

"Right."

"I'll see you then." This was said with a finality that made it clear the exchange was over, and any tenderness that had snuck through was gone. She got in her car and was gone in less than a minute, leaving me in California with the Harpers.

I slowly made my way back to the front door and into the house, feeling as if I was breaking into a secret museum exhibit not meant for my eyes. My suitcase sat off to the side of the gigantic staircase, exactly where Mom had left it. I wanted to carry it up to my bedroom, but I didn't know where that was, or if I even had a bedroom. *Don't just assume anything, Cassidy, you need proof,* I heard Mom say to me. She had been gone five minutes at most, and I was already imagining her voice in my ear.

With this new purpose given by my ever-present mother, I wandered through the house to find someone to ask about sleeping arrangements. Once I reached the dining room I heard the Harpers' voices, and followed the sounds through the French doors and into the kitchen.

Light assaulted me from all directions as I stepped into the room. The positions and pastel shades of the walls were perfect for reflecting sunshine from the giant skylight above. The brightness of the room was matched by the cheery voices of the Harpers, who were all chatting at once as they put away the dishes. I stood there awkwardly, not sure whether to announce my presence, and searched for something new to focus on. I eventually settled on the fancy microwave in the far right corner, and thought about how its wavelengths united to heat up food.

"I'm just saying, I don't know how she does it," Mrs. Harper was saying. "I know that I couldn't just drop off Grace in a different state for the summer. I'd be too worried that something would go wrong or she'd get homesick."

I managed to recall the correct page of my chemistry textbook. *A microwave depends on electromagnetic waves and water molecules*, I recited in my head, studying the control panel of the apparatus.

"Some parents have lots of trust in their children," Mr. Harper said. "And she said that this will be Cassidy's second summer at camp, so she's probably used to it by now." *Water molecules vibrate as they are exposed to alternating electric fields.*

"I'm not saying I don't trust Grace. I just think that Cassidy – oh, Cassidy!" Mrs. Harper exclaimed, noticing that I was standing in the doorway. "Cassidy, did your mother leave?" she asked, dragging me away from my thoughts.

"Yes," I said. "She left a few minutes ago."

"I'm sure you'll miss her!" Mrs. Harper practically cooed, turning her head to one side.

"Yes."

"I promise we'll do our best to make you feel at home," she said warmly, and I gave her a tiny smile in response. I hoped that gesture would end the conversation, but Mrs. Harper kept talking. Her mouth bounced up and down as she moved around the kitchen, saying that Palo Alto was beautiful in the summer, and she hoped I liked home-cooked meals, and they would show me all the best shops around town, and I wasn't to worry because Mr. Harper was going to drive me to Stanford every day. I kept my eyes fixed on the floor and just nodded as much as possible, hoping she didn't think I was being rude.

My eyes roamed again, and after a few loops around the room I noticed Grace, sitting cross-legged on the floor in front of the refrigerator and staring keenly at its doors. She was humming quietly to herself, and now and then she would reach up and pull a magnet off the surface. The magnets were very flat, and from the way they reflected the light, I guessed they were coated with plastic. I watched as she bent one magnet between her fingers while sliding another along the smooth surface of the refrigerator. She seemed to find some great fascination in their movements. I continued to stare, trying to determine the purpose of the activity.

Grace must have noticed I was staring. "Would you like to join me?" she asked.

"Oh, no," I said, backing up a little bit. "I was just watching."

"You sure?" she asked. "It's really fun. You can make some really wacky sentences."

"Excuse me?"

Grace turned the face of one of the magnets toward me, and I saw a word printed on it in lowercase black letters. "You slide the words around the door to create sentences. Then you can rearrange the words in that sentence to make a new one. Just like that! It's like magic," she said, her eyes twinkling.

I couldn't help myself. "You know that's just physics, not magic," I said.

"No, I don't know," she responded. "But I appreciate the thought."

I faltered for a moment. "You're not interested in knowing why you can slide the magnets around? And why they aren't falling?"

"No. I like it when the world's a mystery," Grace said with a shrug. "Then there are fewer things that I have to worry about being under my control. Everything just works."

She turned to look at me, and her bright eyes drilled into mine. I folded my arms over my chest. "I guess."

"It does!"

"I guess."

Grace cocked her head to the side, and there was a moment of silence. The only sound was the clinking of plates that Mr. and Mrs. Harper were loading into the dishwasher. I felt their eyes dart to Grace and me now and then, and wondered if it would be rude for me to leave.

I was sliding surreptitiously back towards the double doors when Grace began to giggle. "You know, you don't need permission to leave the room," she said. I turned back to her, and saw that she was again staring at the magnets on the refrigerator. "This is your house now too."

"She's right," Mrs. Harper said, cutting off my response. "Like I said, we want you to feel at home here."

What was someone supposed to say to that? *Yes, I do* or *Thanks for the thought* or *Sorry, but I really hate it here*? My ability to dredge up a proper response had collapsed under the combined weight of the long drive filled with Mom's lectures, the marathon of forced socialization, and now the experience of standing still while both Mrs. Harper's and Grace's large eyes drilled holes into my face. I felt like one of those poor American sailors, standing at the edge of a ship and waiting for the pirates to make him walk the plank. But instead of sharing that, I swallowed roughly and said, "Really, you don't have to worry about it."

"No, really," Mrs. Harper said. "If you need anything, just tell us."

I need some peace and quiet, and a place where I can be alone with my books. "Okay," I lied. I mentally kicked myself for not having paid more attention during the house tour. As Grace's large eyes continued to bore into my face, I wondered if engineers had ever invented goggles to protect a person from the power of someone else's gaze. If not, then all the goggle inventors of the world needed to meet Grace Harper and get their act together.

After another minute of silent staring, Grace hopped up from the floor. "Come on, I'll show you your room." Mr. Harper was occupying the space between the refrigerator and the door, so Grace tried to crawl between his legs. "Excuse me," she giggled.

Mr. Harper reached down and grabbed Grace, pulling her up into a hug. Grace shrieked and Mr. Harper laughed. I averted my eyes, feeling that I was intruding on a private moment.

"Da-ad," Grace said in a muffled voice. "Let me go! I have to show Cassidy her room."

"Oh, I'm sorry," he said, and I saw that he was grinning. "I thought you said 'Squeeze me.'"

"Da-ad," Grace whined again, and Mr. Harper gave her a big smile before letting her go. She swatted her father's shoulder before skipping over to me. Before I could register what was happening, she grabbed my hand and catapulted me through the dining room.

When we reached the stairs, I gently wrestled my hand free. To avoid any questions from Grace, I acted as though I needed both hands to carry my suitcase. As we trekked up the massive steps, I was once again taken aback by how ornate every aspect of the house was. At the top of the stairs was a doorway into an office that featured a large and intricately carved mahogany desk. *Baroque architecture specialized in covering the inside of a building with intricate carvings*, I remembered. The thought made me ache even more for the familiarity of my books.

"It's pretty, isn't it?" Grace asked, having caught me staring at the desk.

I moved my gaze to hers. "Honestly, it seems like overkill. A desk is there to help you do work. Why make it so fancy?"

Grace giggled again, and I clenched my jaw at yet another display of her unabashed, pointless happiness, thinking that the number of times she had laughed since my arrival was increasing exponentially. Her unabashed, pointless happiness was eating away at my ability to keep up with her antics. *Grace is taking away your grace*, I thought. *How fitting.*

"What is so funny?" I spit out, harsher than I'd meant to be.

"You," she said. "You say funny things." She stepped back down onto the top step, leaned back against the banister, and boosted herself up to sit side-saddle on the steeply sloping handrail. I feared that the force of gravity would overpower her grip and send her sliding precariously to the foot of the stairs. As she balanced and swung her feet back and forth, I noticed that she was wearing a pair of pink rain boots. The girl was wearing rain boots indoors.

"Why are you wearing rain boots?"

"Why not?" Grace replied immediately, not missing a beat.

It was all too much. "Weren't you going to show me my room?" I asked tersely.

"Ah yes. This way!" Grace sang, pushing herself off the stair rail and skipping down a carpeted hallway. I followed her to a wooden door at the very end of the hall. Grace held out her hands in a *ta da!* gesture, as if she was a magician and this door was her main trick. After a minute or so, I realized that she meant for me to enter first. I hesitantly turned the knob, almost afraid of what might lie on the other side. "I hope you like it," she said. "I made up the bed myself."

The style of the room followed the precedent set by the rest of the house. When my eyes landed on the gigantic bed, whose shining wooden frame was obscured by piles of pillows in patterned fabrics, exhaustion coursed through my body like a lightning strike.

"Did you know that you can't wash wool?" a voice said, and it took me a moment to realize that Grace was still in the room.

"I'm sorry, what?"

"Apparently wool can't be washed. Your bed has a wool blanket, and when I was getting the room ready for you I was going to wash all the blankets, but apparently wool has to be dry cleaned." I stared at her as she pulled a stray strand of hair away from her face. "I wish I had known that before I'd washed it," she said with a giggle.

I stared at her as I groped for a rational response. "That's unfortunate," I managed to get out. "Although the blanket probably wishes that more than you do." I rolled my suitcase toward the center of the room before I caught myself and turned back around. "If blankets could wish, that is."

Grace's face twisted. "What?"

"Blankets can't actually wish things."

"But you just said that the blanket probably–"

"I know what I said!" I exclaimed, too loudly. I retreated, horrified at what Mom would say if she had heard me. I flashed back to Mom's voice lecturing about the negative impression that sudden outbursts make, and how I needed to develop better control if I wanted to get good recommendation letters from teachers and do well in college admission interviews. "It … it was personification," I finished as softly as possible, lowering my eyes in contrition. I again noticed Grace's feet and the pink rain boots. They were an annoying shade of pink, I decided. Their brightness made everything else in the room look painfully dull.

never trust a happy song

Unable to look at the boots any longer, I turned away and knelt to open my suitcase and fish out my toiletries bag. I took my time digging through it for my toothbrush, hoping that Grace would leave. But I heard no retreating footsteps, and after I had searched through the bag four times, I realized I still hadn't found my toothbrush.

"Crap," I said as I rose and dropped the bag back into the suitcase.

"What?" Grace asked, hopping over to where I was standing. I turned to find her standing very close to me, and flinched.

"I can't find my toothbrush. I must have forgot to pack it." I rubbed my temple with my fingers, trying to understand how I could have possibly forgotten to pack something as essential as a toothbrush.

"I can lend you one," Grace said. "I have lots of extras!"

"Um ... that's all right," I said, wondering how it was possible for her to sound so excited about toothbrushes. "They can harbor beta-hemolytic streptococcus, and if we swap that bacteria we could get any number of diseases."

Grace sniggered with amusement. "That is the most ridiculous name I have ever heard."

I was about to snap out an explanation of why it was not ridiculous, but in fact very serious, when I was saved by a voice echoing up the stairwell.

"Grace!" someone yelled. "Grace!" I didn't register whose voice it was, nor did I care. I just knew that it was not Grace's, and therefore I was now free. "Have you finished showing Cassidy her room?" the speaker bellowed again.

[*19*]

"Yes!" Grace shouted back. Then her gaze centered on me. "I'll let you rest now. You're probably tired."

"Yes," I said.

"I'll see you tomorrow."

"Yes," I said again, although the thought of having to see this girl every day made me want to scream into one of the bed's many pillows.

Grace skipped out of the room, and I closed the door firmly behind her. Finally free, I ran to the bed that was now mine. Sure enough, beneath the topmost quilt lay a blanket that was oddly puckered and shrunken. I slid down to the bottom edge of the bed and untucked the blanket, searching for the tag. Sure enough, printed in the list of instructions were the words *Dry Clean Only*.

I sighed and tore the blanket completely off the bed, folding it neatly before depositing it in a corner of the room. "Why would I even need two blankets during the summer?" I whispered as I changed into my comfiest sweat pants and climbed back onto the bed. I dropped down onto the pillows and clamped my eyes shut, praying for the oblivion of sleep. However, I was so strung out from the events of the day that settling down was impossible. Every ten seconds or so my forehead twitched, my back itched, or my feet tingled, begging for movement.

After a few more minutes of tossing and turning, I sat up with a sigh and looked around the room again. The fancy wallpaper really was complete overkill. As a rule, I try never to think of a task as impossible, but at that moment I felt extremely doubtful that I'd ever be able to sleep in this new place.

chapter 3

I awoke the next morning to pounding on the door, and shot up in bed as dreadful possibilities flooded my mind. *I'm late for tutoring*, I concluded, and struggled to wrestle free of the blanket wrapped around me. "I'm up, Mom, I'm up!" I yelled, jumping off the bed. My time in the air before my feet hit the floor was twice what it should have been, and I realized something was off.

"I'm not your mother, dear," the voice said from the opposite side of the door. It was Mrs. Harper, and I was in California. I groaned. "Come on down for breakfast," Mrs. Harper went on to say. "I made omelets."

I lumbered over to my still-packed suitcase and began the search for clothes. I wasn't exactly sure what one should wear to breakfast with a family that one met fewer than twenty-four hours before, so I settled on generic jeans and a t-shirt and headed downstairs.

When Mrs. Harper said that she had made omelets, she was seriously understating what awaited me at the table. On each plate sat a gigantic mound of eggs, layered with a series of vegetables and cheese.

"That's a lot of food," I managed to get out as I stared at the creation.

"Your mother said you like eggs for breakfast," Mrs. Harper said as she sashayed around the room, setting a cloth napkin in front of each person.

"I do," I began, and found that I didn't know how to politely continue, so my voice trailed off. I sat down at the table in defeat.

Once all the Harpers were seated at the table, I again became the center of attention.

"So, I'm curious," Mr. Harper said. "Why Stanford? Why did you choose Stanford for your summer studies?"

I was certain Mr. Harper wasn't aware of how complex the answer to that question was, as it didn't just involve summer studies, but also college interviews and resumes and picking a major. "It's a science and math program," I said, giving him the simplest answer. "We study aspects of biology, chemistry, physics, trigonometry, precalculus, and a little calculus." Mr. Harper nodded and I looked down at my plate, hoping I'd be freed from the spotlight. I grasped my fork tightly.

"Wow," Grace said loudly, dragging out the vowel until I practically heard it squeal for mercy. She had come to the table in complete silence, but I sensed that her onslaught of comments was about to begin. "That sounds like a lot of work for the summer!" She took a tiny bite of omelet, and spent a long time chewing it. "What kind of fun things do you want to do during your free time?" she asked once her mouth was empty.

I blinked at her repeatedly before I understood that she really had asked the question, even though the answer seemed so basic. " I hadn't made any plans."

Grace frowned. "Well, there are lots of awesome places we can take you to."

"No, I mean I hadn't planned on doing anything like that."

Grace dropped her fork on her plate, and the collision produced a loud ping. "You mean you're just going to work all the time, *all summer?*"

Apparently Grace was not aware of what the academic summer program entailed. "Well, yes," I said, hoping she hadn't assumed that my staying here meant I'd be able to spend time doing things with her.

"Ew."

If Grace Harper wanted to get on my permanent bad side, she was rapidly succeeding. I gripped my fork harder, and counted the number of days until the beginning of the program.

"That sounds very interesting, Cassidy," Mr. Harper said, distracting me from the hot sensation developing in my frontal vein.

"Thank you. I hope it will be," I said, and then looked back down at my overfilled plate. I had expected the Harpers to keep chattering, but instead a silence fell. *Ah*, I thought. *Finally, something that they do silently.* But when I looked up a few moments later, I found them exchanging glances that were clearly meant to communicate some message about me. Mr. and Mrs. Harper looked concerned, and Grace turned on me with big eyes and a tiny smirk.

"Oh, I'm sorry," I half-said, half-groaned, "was I supposed to supply small talk?"

Grace laughed as though I was her favorite comedian, collapsing forward onto the table and then throwing her head back. "Oh my stars!" she exclaimed, and I wondered if I was supposed to know what that meant. Mr. and Mrs. Harper began to chuckle, and now it was my turn to look around the table, feeling lost.

"I thought that was the end of the conversation," I said in defense, "so I stopped talking." My throat was dry, and I thought I might stutter. "I'm sorry. I'm being rude."

Mrs. Harper gave her husband a look before giving me a warm smile. "It's all right, Cassidy. If you'd rather not say anything while we eat, then that's fine with us."

"I would love that," I said, my voice rising. "Thank you."

"Oh my stars," Grace said again. There was a plunking sound as she dropped her forehead down onto the table. I tilted my head at her, preparing to question her remark, but then realized it would be better to leave it alone.

I did not want to look at the Harpers, because I knew they would probably look uncomfortable, despite their offer of silence. So instead, I returned my gaze to my omelet. As I took in the groupings of chives and cheese across the eggs, I realized that I was incredibly hungry. I cut the omelet into neat little squares, each sized to easily fit into my mouth. *I can fit six pieces length-wise*, I thought, *and four pieces width-wise*. Who could ever eat a twenty-four bite omelet, I wasn't sure, but I dug in anyway.

The Harpers kept their promise, and we ate the rest of our eggs in silence. My plan was to eat my entire omelet, and then excuse myself, needing desperately to return to my room to finish the chapter of math problems remaining from my practice work. After I got to piece twenty I began to lose steam. I stared at the remaining four pieces, frustrated that they were standing between me and my work.

"You don't have to eat it all," Mrs. Harper said, and I felt my cheeks grow warm.

"Well, I wanted to …." *Go back to my room*, I finished in my head, but again I didn't know how to say it politely.

"Really, it's okay," she said. Then she began to laugh. "Goodness, you look like a deer caught in headlights. It's all right, I promise. If you're done, you can take your plate to the kitchen."

"I'll show her," Grace chirped, hopping out of her seat.

"Oh, it's okay," I began, but before I could finish the sentence, Grace grabbed my plate with one hand and laced her other hand in mine, pulling me out of my chair. "Come on," she said, and skipped out of the dining room.

I couldn't help myself. "Why are you skipping?"

"Because it's fun!" she said, hopping even higher. "You should try."

"But there's no need," I said, shaking my head as I was dragged along.

Once we reached the kitchen counter, Grace stopped and did a pirouette, slinging my dish into the sink as she turned. Then she stopped and looked straight into my eyes. "There doesn't have to be a need for everything, Cassidy."

I didn't know how to respond to that, so I just looked down. Eventually I heard Grace retreat into the dining room. I had only been up for an hour, and I already felt completely overwhelmed – a feeling that I was not used to experiencing outside the context of assignments, tests, projects, and deadlines. In fact, my stomach ached at the lack of those elements, as being overwhelmed by academia was much more comfortable than this social distress. I tiptoed back around to the staircase and then sprinted the rest of the way to my room, seeking solace in my books.

Although I needed to finish the rest of my practice problems, I found myself reaching for my beloved United States history textbook, which I had managed to sneak into my suitcase after Mom had already checked its contents. U.S. history is normally a class for juniors, but Mom had convinced my counselor to enroll me in it as a sophomore. It had been love at first sight. I had never read anything as fascinating as the story of how an entire country came together and stumbled and grew, through the endless work and mistakes of a group of dedicated people. If people like George Washington, Rosa Parks, and Abraham Lincoln were able to survive the long march to create a strong and equal country, then I should surely be able to survive the long march to college.

I flipped the textbook open and paged through the chapters, running a finger along their worn edges. I stopped on my favorite section, which was about the events that led to the Union and the Confederacy declaring war against each other. The times were filled with violence and disagreements, but I found reassurance in their existence. These events were proof that people were passionate and full of life. They were proof that people would fight for what they believed in. And, despite all of the conflict, the United States was still standing.

I skipped ahead to the section about John Brown, the determined man who participated in the bloody fight to make Kansas a slave-free state. He later led a violent invasion of the South, during which he killed many innocent people. John Brown believed in fighting for what is important, even if there are casualties along the way. Despite his good intentions, he was arrested for murder and treason, and declared insane. I scanned down to my favorite paragraph, about his trial and hanging. Brown stayed completely silent throughout the entire process, even when they brought him up to the gallows and wrapped his neck in a noose. He didn't try to fight for his innocence, or point out the inconsistencies in the justice system. But nothing is more tragic and haunting than his last words – "This *is* a beautiful country." I wanted desperately to know if they were honest or sarcastic – a comment on how America had let him down, or a testament to how the country was beautiful anyway. And if the latter, I wanted to know what that beauty was. My mind began to wander as I imagined the possible formulations of that kind of beauty.

The tension from the breakfast encounter slowly faded away, and I became aware of activity around me. I heard the faint sound of running water, perhaps coming from the bathroom next to my room. I heard the clanking of dishes from below, which was probably from Mrs. Harper in the kitchen. The sun shone brightly through the unshaded windows, and birds flew to and fro in the tree nearest my bedroom. Life was going on all around me, a beautiful but sad reminder that I needed to stop procrastinating and get on with my own. I sighed and closed the history book, dismissing all thoughts of John Brown. My mind was quiet for one beautiful minute, before I pulled out my math problem set and began my assault on precalculus.

chapter *4*

At first I had opposed the idea of attending summer programs. I was already used to centering my life around school, but that additional step seemed extreme. I had begun taking extra after-school classes in sixth grade, and then after eighth grade Mom pulled me out of my old public school in favor of a more demanding program at a private school. After this switch, I was submerged in a completely new mindset. Our teachers reminded us daily that any low grade could compromise our entire future, by making us lag behind our peers forever in the race for success. It took only a few days for me to accept this as truth.

By the middle of sophomore year, it was already hard for me to remember what I did with my free time in middle school. I never was big on sleepovers, and I no longer spent time hanging out with friends during the afternoons and weekends. If an activity wouldn't bolster my future, it wasn't on my agenda. "Pain before gain," Mom always said. Usually this made sense to me. But now and then I wondered if the pain would ever end, or if we will just live in a perpetual state of pain for future gain until we die.

Having arrived in Palo Alto on a Friday, I had to wait two days before the Stanford program began. I spent most of that time seeking refuge in my new room, trying to avoid interaction with the Harpers. They were nice people, but perhaps *too* nice. I wondered if they really liked me, or were just being kind because they felt obligated. For example, after waking up on Sunday morning, I immediately resumed working on my math packet. I was wading through the proof of an especially complicated identity when Mrs. Harper knocked on my door, calling me downstairs for breakfast. When I refused in what I hoped was a polite manner, I thought that would be the end of it. But no, she came back a few minutes later with a plate holding enough food to power me through the rest of the weekend, and set it on my bedside table. Although the smells wafting from the warm plate made my stomach do somersaults, I didn't eat it. I didn't know whether I was allowed to eat on the bed, or if I was required to eat everything on the plate, or where to put the plate when I was done, so it seemed safer to just not touch the plate at all.

After forty-eight hours in my room, I was especially excited on Monday morning when it was finally safe for me to emerge from my cave. I packed my backpack with the binder of practice work plus all of my own textbooks, not knowing which ones I would need. The familiar weight of the bag on my right shoulder sent joy down my spine, and made the ride in the car with Mr. Harper almost bearable.

"Grace really wanted to come along and see you off," Mr. Harper said as he revved up the engine. "But she has diving practice right now."

"Diving?" I asked, picturing Grace scuba-diving to study Pacific Ocean marine life.

"Yes," Mr. Harper responded, his voice warm. "As in swimming."

"Oh," I said, frowning. And, as the conversation had now left my area of expertise, I had nothing else to say.

When Mr. Harper pulled up in front of the camp orientation headquarters, my spirits lifted. I gazed around at the buildings, seeing a mirror image of the brochure photos lining the wall of my room at home. "It's a lovely campus, isn't it?" Mr. Harper said as he parked the car and turned so that I could see his face. "I think you'll really enjoy your time here."

"I know I will," I responded.

"Oh?"

"Yes. I've been looking forward to this for a while." I could tell from the look on Mr. Harper's face that he wanted to respond, but I managed to pull the minivan door open and exit the car before he could speak. "Thank you for dropping me off, Mr. Harper," I said, dipping my head slightly.

"You're welcome," he said with a voice that didn't match the puzzlement on his face. "Just call me when you're done, and I'll come pick you up."

"Okay," I said. I thanked him one last time before feeling that it was proper for me to turn my back and walk speedily toward the familiar buildings.

It took me twenty minutes to register and get directions to the appropriate lecture hall. During the process, a cheery student gave me a printed copy of the program schedule. It was organized into a rather poorly sectioned chart, but I figured out that my first class of the day was an introductory seminar. *Not exactly educational*, the Mom voice said. However, I had felt so out of place since my arrival that anything with the word 'seminar' in its title sounded like heaven. I felt certain that there I would meet people who spoke the same language as I did.

have the word *genes*, which sounds the same, but refers to the biological structures. Which, I might add, can also be unzipped by DNA helicase, much in the way that pick-up line boy would be saying he wants to unzip his beloved's jeans."

"That's horrible," I said, finding it difficult to believe he was serious.

"But rational," the boy added, pointing a finger at me.

"Fine, I'll give you that."

"Time's up, people!" I heard the professor say, and we both turned to see him standing on the stage with his arms outstretched. "You may now be wondering whether this little exercise had a point." He paused as if waiting to hear the 'yes' that we were all thinking. "The note cards served two purposes. The first was to be an icebreaker, so that each of you could introduce yourself to at least one other person. The second was to show the importance of communication skills. Over the next few months it is imperative that you not only work hard and complete your assignments, but also communicate well with your classmates. Communication skills will be important throughout your professional life, no matter what profession you ultimately choose. You will need to be able to communicate effectively both orally and with the written word." Here the professor paused and scanned the room slowly. "So, perhaps I should be more blatant. That means that if you have not already introduced yourself to your partner, please do so now."

"I guess that's us," the boy said, swinging his lower body around so that it faced mine.

"I guess," I said, mimicking his movement in a much less graceful manner. "I'm Cassidy."

"And my name is La Keith. Pleased to meet you."

"La Keith?" I repeated. The name did not at all match the boy sitting before me. "That's an odd name."

The boy groaned. "No, it isn't. You're thinking of it spelled the American way." He flipped over his notecard and wrote on the back of it. "See," he said, gesturing for me to come closer. "It's spelled like this: L-I-K-I-T-H. Likith."

I studied the paper with furrowed eyebrows. "That looks like it's pronounced 'Lick it.'"

"Not in Hindi."

"Oh."

I pushed the card back to Likith and then scooted back into my chair. We stared at each other, drumming our feet against the floor.

"Should we shake hands?" I asked.

"I don't think that would be appropriate for the situation at hand," Likith said, his words accompanied by a flurry of movements from his left hand.

"Valid," I said, mentally discarding the idea.

"But, what the hell!" he said, throwing both hands up into the air. "This is a science and math program, and part of being scientific is being willing to experiment, right?" He stretched his very thin arm out toward mine, so far that I had to bend my arm at the elbow and then flex my hand in order to meet his. We shook three times.

"Moving right along," the professor said, interrupting us mid-shake. "Now that you've all introduced yourselves, it's time for me to do the same. I am Professor Deal, your main lecturer for this program. Each morning you will report to me and hand in the work that is due that day. I expect only the best from you, and this includes never blowing off an assignment. Slacking off is unacceptable, as it means that you are not learning all that you can. And what is the point of our being here, if we are not here to learn and fulfill our full potential?"

As he gave this speech, a hard edge crept into Professor Deal's voice. By the time he spoke about his expectation of never missing an assignment, his tone was almost threatening. But none of us flinched at the change. It wasn't anything we hadn't heard before.

At that moment, I realized I was able to use the word *we* when referring to the people around me, even though I didn't know them. By virtue of our mutual presence in this room, I already felt closer to them than to anyone else I had met since leaving home. I felt tension leave my body as I took in Professor Deal's words, my brain kicking into its normal gear and preparing to learn.

chapter 5

I avoided leaving Stanford until six in the evening, when a library worker noticed I wasn't a college student and ordered me to leave. Mr. Harper drove me home, thankfully in silence, and I was able to sneak into the house and up the stairs without being asked any questions about how the day had gone. I hated the classic first-day-of-school questions. Asking them wouldn't even make sense, since I wasn't technically going to school. But the Harpers seemed like just the kind of family who would ask them anyway.

I opened my bedroom door to find myself face to face with Grace, her large eyes so close to mine that I felt they might pop out at me.

"Hi," she said pleasantly, waggling her fingers hello as she popped my bubble of silence. "How was your first day of school?"

Here we go. "It was fine," I said, not feeling up to an explanation.

"Good!" Grace chirped. "I was just making your room more home-y while you were gone. I hope you don't mind."

"Homier," I said delicately, trying to slip away from her gaze. "And it's fine." I squeezed past her body, avoiding eye contact as much as possible. That's when I noticed the window seat.

"What are those?" I asked, freezing mid-squeeze.

"Candles," Grace said, her unspoken *duh* hanging in the air.

"Why did you put candles in my room?" I asked, whipping around to face her.

"They smell like mint," Grace said, her eyes opening even wider. "They're supposed to relieve stress." Her words were so kind that I almost didn't continue, but a gut reaction drove me forwards.

"I'm not allowed to have candles," I blurted, trying to make my eyes as expressive as hers. Maybe Grace and I could master the art of subliminally communicating through wide gazes, and then we'd never have to speak.

Grace let out a hushed giggle. "What? That's ridiculous. My parents don't have any rules against candles."

"Yes, but *my* parents do," I said, feeling the panic rising. "I mean, my mom …." I breathed in and tried to slow down. "Candles can slowly kill you."

"What?" Grace repeated, her laugh now bold. "Candles can't kill you. Not unless you use them to set a fire."

"No," I said, straightening up. "Candles need oxygen to burn. When you light a candle, you feed the flame the oxygen you need for yourself. The flame depletes the air, and eventually it's going to be bad for you. No one wins."

"Oh my stars," Grace said, leaning her head against the door in a manner I found very irritating. "Listen, Cassidy. There might be some very small chance of that happening, but that is no reason not to burn candles!"

"Can you just take them away?" I asked. Somewhere down the hall footsteps sounded, and my heart rate jumped. "*Please*?"

"Okay, okay, I'll take them away," Grace said, the words merely an accompaniment to her laugh. "Geez, Cassidy."

"Thank you," I said, watching as Grace pranced across the room and scooped up the unlit candles. "And I need to get started on my homework now. So do you think you could … maybe … leave?" I struggled with each word, spreading the syllables out.

"Sure," Grace said. She began to hum a tune as she walked across the room, and paused when she reached the door. "Remember, dinner's in half an hour."

"Right," I said, staring at the floor. As soon as Grace left, I turned to unpacking. My earlier attempts to retrieve items from the bottom of the suitcase had created a mess on the floor like a map of clothing countries and carpet oceans. As I neatly tucked my clothing away in drawers, the room started to look like it could be mine. With everything put away, cleaning was no longer a viable form of procrastination, and I turned to my backpack. Leafing through handouts on physics and precalculus, I eventually found the assignment on vectors. "A vector is magnitude plus direction," I quietly recited to myself, "while a secant is a value that just describes something's magnitude." I became completely enveloped in a world of magnitude and distance, a state only broken when I heard a knock on the door.

"Cassidy," Grace sang from the other side. "Dinner!"

"Oh, right!" I said, removing the papers from my lap. "I'm sorry, I got distracted." I hastily opened the door and ran into the hallway. "I hope your parents won't be angry."

"What?" Grace said, giving me a look.

I stared at her for a second. "What?" I countered.

never trust a happy song

She shook her head. "You say the most ridiculous things. No, they're not angry. You're fine."

"Okay."

"My stars," Grace said, rolling her eyes as we continued down the hallway. I stared after her, again confused as to why the stars were hers.

Mrs. Harper had made a feast for dinner. Dishes of food covered most of the table surface. I stared at the banquet in awe.

"Look good?" Mrs. Harper asked as she and the rest of the family settled into their chairs.

"It's so much," I blurted, and I heard Grace giggle.

"Don't worry, Cassidy," Mrs. Harper said with a little smile. "You don't have to eat it all."

"Did you make all this?" I asked, the calculations in my brain overriding what Mrs. Harper had been saying.

"Yes."

"That must have taken forever!" I said, my eyes growing wider.

Mrs. Harper looked thoroughly amused. "Please, Cassidy, sit down."

"That's so much time," I said, partly to myself, sitting down slowly.

"I enjoy cooking." Mrs. Harper said, now looking directly at me.

"Oh," I said. "All right, I understand." I didn't.

We ate in silence for a while, until Mr. Harper took a break from his chicken and cleared his throat. "Are you going bowling tonight, Grace?" he asked after dabbing at his mouth with a napkin.

"Monroe can't go," Grace said, with no napkin covering her mouth even though it was just as full, "so I wasn't going to."

"Why can't he go?" Mrs. Harper asked, and I put down my fork since it seemed we were taking a collective break from eating.

"His dad is making him stay home every night this week and work on his summer reading," Grace said, her face twisted as if reading was the world's biggest and ugliest insect. "He's afraid that if Monroe doesn't get a jump on it now, he'll never do it."

"Well, that's probably a wise decision," Mrs. Harper said, the personification of sympathy. "But I'm sorry you won't get to go. I know how much you enjoy your bowling nights."

"Why doesn't Cassidy go with you?" Mr. Harper said, joining in suddenly. I jumped at the mention of my name, its vocalization converting me from an audience member to a cast member who did not know her lines. My face grew hot as all eyes focused on me.

"Oh, no, really, I ...." I trailed off, struggling with the act of speaking and trying to control my heart rate at the same time. "I'm not really that into bowling. Plus I have so much work to do. I can't get behind on the first day."

Mrs. Harper tilted her head at me. "I know you have a lot of work, Cassidy. But there's no reason you shouldn't be able to take a few hours off. It is summer, after all."

"I'm sorry, I just don't think that's an advisable plan," I said, and then realized that I was apologizing to the wrong person. "I'm sorry," I repeated, but this time to Grace. Her brown eyes were now a size I hadn't known to be biologically possible, and her lips formed a puppy dog pout.

never trust a happy song

"Please?" she whimpered. "It's a lot of fun."

"I ... I'm sorry but ...." The words *I can't* were on the tip of my tongue, but Grace's incredibly sad face cut through my resolve like hydrochloric acid. "Okay," I said with a groan, ashamed that I had caved. Mom would be disappointed. "But not tonight, okay?"

"So tomorrow?" Grace asked, her puppy dog eyes still shining in all their glory.

"Well ...." I cleared my throat, staring at a wall of hesitation. "That's not really good either."

"The day after that?" Grace asked, leaning forward in her chair.

"You see, it's just–"

"After that?"

"Grace, if you would just–"

"After *that*?"

"Ugh, fine! We can go Friday!" I exploded, slamming my hands onto the table. Mr. and Mrs. Harper both looked alarmed, while Grace looked downright amused. "We can go Friday," I repeated more calmly, adjusting my volume to a level appropriate for the dinner table. I tried to smile to cover up the slip, but my muscles felt too heavy to move.

"Awesome," Grace said, wearing the grin of a lion about to savor its prey. Then she looked down at her plate, which I noted with astonishment to be empty. "May I be excused?" she asked after a moment of contemplation.

"You may," Mrs. Harper replied, looking a bit shaken after the shouting match. I looked down at my lap to avoid their eyes, but was still very aware of Grace as she pranced out of the dining room. The echo of her presence reached us long after she was gone.

chapter 6

On Wednesday I received the first anxious e-mail message from Mom. *Hi Cassidy*, it read. *I am sure that you have settled in well at the Harpers'. I hope that they are a good host family for you, and won't distract you too much from your studies. I trust camp is going well. Remember, just let me know if you need any help! Love you, Mom.* It was short, to the point, and totally my mother. As I stared at the words on the phone screen, I wondered if getting roped into going bowling was consistent with not letting the Harpers distract me from my studies.

Although I was not normally a fan of group work, I found an unexpectedly excellent partner in Likith. He was very focused, albeit with a scientific pick-up line or two, and was quick to comprehend complex mathematical concepts. Even better, he was willing to explain them to me without making me feel like I should be banished to the bottom of the barrel of potential talent. By unspoken agreement, we sat next to each other even when a problem set wasn't that difficult. We were both willing to work in complete silence, and that made us the perfect blend.

On Friday, I found it strangely difficult to focus on our trigonometry assignment. To improve my concentration, I tried blinking vigorously, a tactic I used during the school year to prevent myself from falling asleep. By doing this, I could slowly make each sentence come into focus. *This ... figure ... is ... a ... representation ... of ...*

"Whoa, do you have a bug in your eye or something?" Likith asked at one point during the blink-fest.

"No," I said, my annoyance coloring the word. "I'm just so distracted and I don't know why."

"And the answer to distraction is to blink like you're suffering an epileptic fit?" Likith said, raising his eyebrows.

"No," I said again, my glare in full blaze. Moments like these made me remember why I had initially hated him. "I'm just trying to snap my eyes out of it." This made Likith laugh. I frowned, realizing that it did sound rather stupid. "It works when I'm at risk of falling asleep," I muttered, returning in defeat to the trigonometry in front of me.

"Don't sweat it," Likith said. "Everyone has those days. If you aren't able to finish the work now, just do it this evening when you get home."

"I can't," I said, my grip tightening on my pencil.

"Why not?"

"I'm going bowling," I said, my voice purposely unintelligible.

"What?"

"I'm going bowling, all right?"

Likith momentarily tried to repress his laughter, but then burst out in snickers. "*Bowling*? For God's sakes why?"

"Because the crazy daughter of my host family apparently loves to go bowling, and her friend who normally accompanies her can't go because he's staying home to work, which is what *I* should be doing!" The words came out in a rush, relieved to finally escape my head.

"That was definitely a run-on sentence," Likith said, amusement coloring his face and voice. I swiveled to fix him with my best glare,

never trust a *happy* song

but he cut it off by holding up his hands. "I'm sorry, that must be frustrating," he said. "Why don't you just explain to her that you don't have time for activities like bowling?"

"I did!" I said, channeling my frustration into a death grip on my pencil. "At least, I tried! But she doesn't understand. I mean, what can you do when you try to explain something to someone and they don't understand?"

Likith shrugged. "Try again?"

"Why?" I spit out, cutting off the end of his last word. "Why should I have to?" I let go of my pencil with a sigh and felt the relief in my finger joints. "A theorem has an irrefutable proof. An equation doesn't argue back if it doesn't like how you went about proving it. As long as you reach the right conclusion, it's happy. Why can't people be like that?"

Likith's expression became pained. "Honestly, I don't know. I never had to take a class on people."

"Ugh, some genius you are!" I said with a small smile.

"Sorry," Likith said, actually looking a little ashamed.

I spaced out for a moment, my vision blurring until a completed thought snapped me back to reality. "She's just so happy," I said, feeling like I had just answered the last question on a really hard test. "Not just happy, but *perky*. I mean, *I'm* happy. But being happy does not mean I have to be that perky and ...," I paused, my vocabulary for these kinds of descriptions rather rusty, "... out there."

Amusement rippled across Likith's face before he tried to fake composure. "So, this girl really pushes your buttons, huh?"

I observed his sudden change in demeanor with confusion, and then grimaced. "Please don't tell me this is making you think of a pick-up line."

"Yes," Likith said, and I could tell he was suppressing laughter. "But don't worry. I feel this one is too primitive to share with you."

"Oh no, whatever shall I do," I muttered, turning my attention back to my worksheet. "I forget, what's the derivative of $\sin x \cos x$?"

"That would just be negative $\cos x \sin x$. If you forget, you can always find it using the product rule."

"Oh, thanks," I said, feeling dumb for having forgotten such basic calculus.

"Hey, Cassidy," Likith said after a minute or two.

"What, Likith?"

"If I were $\sin^2 x$, and you were $\cos^2 x$, then together we would be one." I glared at Likith's beaming face before turning back to the problems at hand.

I tried to slow time, but due to my lack of superpowers, the moment for my outing with Grace did eventually arrive. Grace came into my room after dinner, wearing a combination of colors I'd never before seen on a human.

"*What* are you wearing?" she screeched, as I considered the exact same question about her.

I diverted my attention from her body to mine. "A pair of jeans and a t-shirt," I said, looking back up. "What's wrong with that?"

"It's so plain!" Grace exclaimed. "So boring! Come on, we're going *bowling*! At least put on some plaid or polka dots or something."

never trust a happy song

I raised an eyebrow. "I didn't realize bowling required special attire."

Grace sighed and perched her hand on her hip. "Normally, when Monroe and I go, we wear our most hideously colorful outfits. Bowling is such a goofy activity that you have to feel goofy in order to do it right." Grace walked over and leaned down so close to my face that I could smell the watermelon gum she was chewing. "You have to feel the goofy."

"*Feel* the *goofy?*" I repeated. "Please tell me you are kidding."

"Nope," she said with a little bounce that sent her hair flying.

"What if you run into people you know at the bowling alley?"

Grace scoffed at me. "So?" She gave the word so much weight that I felt I had already lost the argument.

"All right!" I said, throwing my hands up. "Let's go bowl."

Grace smiled brightly and grabbed my hand, which I found as unpleasant as ever. "This is going to be so much fun."

"If you say so," I muttered, wondering what Mom would say if she saw me being dragged out of my room by a girl who had been thrown up on by a rainbow.

chapter 7

Halfway through the drive, I realized that I had never been to a bowling alley before. Being so unprepared made me feel even more uncomfortable, and I squirmed in my seat.

"If you have fun," Grace said, "which I *know* you will, then this should become a permanent thing. I mean, just going with Monroe is fun and all, but I love the idea of a bowling trio! And I think you'd really like Monroe. He's a nice guy, if you can overlook his addiction to violent video games." I peered over at Grace in time to see her roll her eyes with a smile. I tried to imagine the boy who would be best friends with this weird girl, and go bowling with her in multicolored outfits. The picture never came.

As Mr. Harper dropped us off at the bowling alley, Grace once again grabbed my hand, and I realized that as long as I was with her, I would probably be dragged everywhere. Grace gave Mr. Harper a goodbye kiss on the cheek before propelling us towards the building. It was square and black, with a neon sign that read "Lots o' Lanes." The whole setup looked rather uninviting.

"What's your shoe size?" Grace asked once we got inside.

"Uh, 7," I said, wondering what shoes had to do with bowling. Before I could inquire, Grace had dashed over to a Formica-clad counter. I watched as she talked animatedly to the man behind the desk, her hair dancing in tandem with her mouth. Soon she turned to skip back to me, two neon pairs of shoes dangling from her hands. *Why does everything have to be neon?* I lamented.

never trust a *happy* song

My palms started to sweat, and I wished I had a pencil with me. But I wasn't able to focus on that for long, for Grace wound our hands together and raced toward one of the bowling lanes. She catapulted me into a seat and dropped a pair of shoes in my lap. They looked very uncomfortable.

"What are these for?"

Grace gave me a look. "To *wear*." I nodded and she turned her attention to her own shoes before flipping back around. "Wait. Don't tell me you have *never gone bowling before!*" she exclaimed like I had never breathed. I winced, fearing her wrath, and forced myself to nod 'yes.'

"Oh my stars," she cried, throwing her hands up.

The sweat on my palms made them itch. "Grace–"

"No, no," she said. "The learner does not speak. The learner just observes. You are in bowling school now, girlfriend."

"O-okay," I said, wincing at the pet name. *Girlfriend* sounded like a greeting used at cheer camp. Truthfully, I had no idea what went on at cheer camp, but *girlfriend* matched the exchanges I had created in my head. I wasn't a girlfriend. I was simply a girl, or a friend, but the two together created cacophony.

"Hello-o," Grace whined, passing her hand in front of my face. "Earth to Cassidy. Anyone home?"

"Yes, Grace," I said as gently as possible. I was almost certain that this would not be the kind of lesson I enjoyed. But figuring I should give her the benefit of the doubt, I assumed my normal learning mindset. *Think of this as just another lecture at Stanford*, I thought to myself, straightening up as best as possible in the bowling alley's molded plastic chairs.

Grace skipped over to a row of shelves containing bowling balls of all colors. *Subject is choosing which color she wishes to use*, I reported to myself, imagining that I was writing this down in my notebook. Grace picked up and put down exactly ten bowling balls before she settled on a bright lime green one. *Through trial and error, subject identifies the optimal choice of color, and now proceeds to the lane*, I reported. *Mode of transportation: skipping.* Grace positioned herself in front of the lane, standing on one of the many lines drawn on the floor. I remembered having seen bowling championships on TV, so I anticipated the normal series of steps required to properly aim and release the ball. But Grace didn't simply step forward – she danced. *Subject performs an odd combination of prancing and spinning. Subject jerks her arm forward and releases the ball. Ball immediately lands in the gutter.*

Grace was horrible at bowling. That conclusion was blindingly clear after watching her repeat this process five more times. Every single time, she flung the ball at an angle not parallel to the lane, guaranteeing that it would fly to the side and land in the gutter. She was an insult to physics.

"Grace," I said quietly, standing up from my chair. "Your ball is going straight into the gutter."

Grace shrugged. "I know."

"Well, did you know that there is an easy way to ensure that you knock down all the pins every time?" I said, life returning to my voice. Grace stared at me blankly, so I continued. "See, it all depends on your direction of initial force and direction of action. Right now, your direction of initial force is at an angle such that your ball inevitably goes into the gutter. But," I said, and here I approached the lane and demonstrated with my arms, "if you were to release the ball along a line parallel to the gutter, then all your force would be focused on sending the ball straight towards the pins." I mimicked this movement with my hands. "Now all that matters is the vertical impetus that you will give to the ball. This can be calculated through simple trigonometry. But since we want the ball to go straight and far, I estimate that an angle of negative forty-five degrees will deliver good results."

I grabbed Grace's bowling ball and, feeling its weight, hypothesized the amount of force that would be needed. Then I swung my right hand back and, after taking a few steps forward, brought my hand forward in a perfectly straight line and let go. The ball eventually collided with the middle pin, sending all of them to the ground. I couldn't help smiling.

"Okay, now why don't you t–," I began, turning back to Grace. But I stumbled to a halt when I saw the anger painted across her face.

"Why are you doing this?" she asked, her words clipped, all trace of a song gone from her voice.

"What do you mean?"

She blew up her bangs with a puff of air. "Why are you trying to turn this into something that is about physics?"

"I'm not trying, I mean ...," I trailed off, her sudden seriousness making it hard for me to think. "Bowling *is* about phys–"

"No!" she almost yelled, pointing her finger at me. "No, it doesn't have to be. But that's just the first thing you think of, isn't it?"

"I'm just trying to help you."

"And *I'm* trying to help *you*!" My mouth opened and closed several times, but the sudden dryness of my tongue prevented words from forming. "The point of this isn't to figure out how to get a strike through physics or whatever," Grace continued. "The point is to not care what people around you are thinking and just be goofy, have fun, laugh!"

"That's not something I really want to do," I managed to get out. Grace rolled her eyes again, and I suddenly felt very angry. "Why are you giving me such a hard time?" I yelled. "You forced me to do this with you!"

"Yes, and I was hoping you'd be willing to at least *try* to have fun. Are you even capable of having fun?" When I didn't answer, she threw up her hands. "Oh my stars!"

"Okay," I said seriously, having reached my limit. "You need to stop saying that."

"Excuse me?" Grace countered, and we were now both full-on yelling. Our argument was beginning to attract the attention of people in adjacent lanes. Normally that would have terrified me, but I was so angry that there was no room for fear.

"You can't say 'Oh my stars.' 'Oh my stars' is not a thing, and it makes no sense. The whole point of that saying is that you're calling out to someone for help, and stars are not 'someone,' and certainly not capable of helping." The words were out and gone before I realized what was happening. Grace just stared back at me, and I wanted so badly to shake the girl and make her realize that life couldn't be all overalls and pink rain boots and guardian stars. I wanted to make her realize that sometimes you had to work.

By this point we had drawn some serious attention to ourselves. In my peripheral vision I saw that a group of girls our age had positioned themselves at the lane next to ours. They were clustered together, all standing with their hips jutting out to the side, and staring.

"Well, what do you know," one of them said. "It's Grace, and she's actually holding her own in an argument." Something about the girl's tone made my spine tingle. "That's something I never thought I'd see," she continued with a laugh. The tingle bounced up and down my spine like an electric signal, and I turned away from Grace's gaze to study the speaker. She was tall and thin with wispy hair, wearing an outfit that could have passed as a prep school uniform. Her friends were dressed in the same style, wearing a plaid button down shirt with pants or a skirt.

"Looks like Grace the Disgrace found someone besides that idiotic boy to go bowling with her," one of the other girls said with a smirk. "Surprising."

"More surprising is the fact that she was actually willing to take off those rain boots," a third girl added in a taunting voice. She leaned toward us, all her weight slanted on one hip. "Maybe she actually figured out that it's not going to rain in California in the *summer*."

It took me a moment to add up the girls' fiery eyes, pointed stares, and biting words, and realize what was happening. I turned to look at Grace, and saw that her face had lost whatever anger it had held before. Now she just looked sad. And even though I had only known her for a week, I had already classified her as someone who could never, ever look sad. Her eyes had grown huge and sparkly, and her mouth had dropped its normal smile.

"Hi, guys," she said. "What's up?"

"What's up is that your outfit is an insult to well-dressed people everywhere," the first girl said. Without thinking, I whipped back to face her, alarmed by the rush of hate that flooded through me. This girl was definitely nothing but mean.

Grace began to stutter a response, but whatever she had been trying to say was cut off by another round of laughter. Stuck in a game of verbal ping pong, I slowly turned back to her, almost scared of what I'd see. Grace's eyes were pointed down, but her head was at such an angle that I knew she wasn't just studying her shoes. "Let's go," she whispered after a moment. She turned robotically to head for the shoe counter, and it took me a moment to realize why I was not moving as well. For the first time all day, Grace had not grabbed my hand.

"Bye-bye, Grace the Disgrace," one of the Mean Girls sing-songed after us as we walked away. When I caught up with Grace at the counter, she dropped to a crouch and removed her shoes. I took that as a cue that I should take off mine too. After we returned the bowling shoes, I sat down to put my original footwear back on. But Grace just stood right up and kicked the bowling alley's double doors open, her boots still dangling from her hands. I followed silently as she walked outside and into the parking lot, the dust of the concrete parking lot sticking to the bottoms of our bare feet.

chapter 8

I had never before found silence to be unbearable, but during the car ride back from the bowling alley, all I wanted was for someone to speak. The unspoken words pressed down like a new form of gravity. Grace was a different person, leaning over so that her hair fell in front of her face. Mr. Harper had not said anything since he asked how the bowling had gone. Perhaps he sensed that something was wrong. All I wanted was to ask Grace what had happened in the bowling alley, and why those girls had been so mean to her, but it felt like Grace was the only one who could cut through this silence. When we finally reached the house, I trailed behind Grace as she walked upstairs. When we reached the landing, she ran to the bathroom, closing the door quietly behind her. Not knowing where else to go, I reverted to my usual routine, going straight to my room and pulling out a packet of physics problems. I began to work.

As I tried to think through the problems, the image of Grace's sad face kept invading my thoughts. In that moment she had looked so foreign, and it seemed impossible that such a transformation could have happened so quickly. I had never thought that there might be another aspect to Grace, a side of her personality that wasn't on the surface. I had assumed that, like a specimen under a microscope, I had seen all of her within a few days. But now she was different, and I had no explanation for the phenomenon.

I remained in this state of mind for the entirety of the weekend. I didn't know how to deal with the feelings – whether to turn to my mother, or Likith, or to approach Grace. The first option didn't seem very wise, as I could already play out in my head the conversation that would take place if I asked Mom about something so nonacademic in nature. And that lack of connection to school was what made my fascination incredibly frustrating. Grace was just one person out of hundreds in my life – one single person. And yet one insignificant fact about her had stuck in my mind like a scared animal, digging its claws in deeper the more I tried to make it let go. *It shouldn't matter*, I told myself. *She probably just doesn't do well in school.* The problem with that reasoning was that it led to the question of *Why?*

"Is it going to look good on your college resume?" the Mom voice said. "No? Then forget it. It isn't valuable for your future, and therefore it doesn't merit contemplation."

Discussing the matter with Likith wasn't an option at the moment, as I was not at camp and we had not established other methods of communication. That left the third option: approach Grace. I was trying to assemble the appropriate question to ask, when the door flew open and derailed my train of thought.

In slunk a scraggy boy, clad all in grey, from his hooded sweatshirt to the pattern of his athletic shoes. Though his clothes were subdued, his presence automatically made everything in the room seem dimmer by comparison. "'Sup," he said, seemingly to no one in particular. I bit down on my tongue, already feeling the need to flee.

"Hello," I responded timidly. He turned to stare directly at me and I stared back. And then he continued to stare. I stayed locked in the laser beam of his gaze for maybe a minute, until I felt on the verge of explosion. "Who are you?" I asked, hoping I was not overstepping the boundaries of propriety, given that he was a stranger and this was technically my room.

"Who are *you*?" the boy shot back, bringing his right hand up to adjust his glasses.

"I'm Cassidy," I said. I didn't believe in realistic dreams, but I surreptitiously pinched myself to make sure I hadn't drifted off into an unplanned nap.

"Oh," the boy said. "Well, 'sup Cassidy." His eyes wandered off before shooting back to me a moment later. "Why are you here?"

"This is my room."

Monroe looked around, seemingly startled. "No way! Are Grace's parents taking in foreign boarders or something?"

I could already tell that this boy and I weren't going to be friends. "What?" I exclaimed. "That's the most ridiculous th–"

"Chill," he said, holding his hand out. His voice became more serious. "It was a joke. I know you're not really an exchange student." I stared at him blankly until he sighed. "I was just trying to lighten the mood."

"Well, it wasn't funny."

"Point taken," he said, nodding his pointer finger in my direction.

By now I had lost all patience, so instead of trying a new tactic, I recycled my earlier question. "*Who are you?*"

"I'm Monroe," the boy said, walking forward and holding out his hand.

"Cassidy," I said, accepting his implicit request to shake hands.

"You'd already told me that," Monroe said with a wink, "but I appreciate the proper introduction." An unpleasant feeling spread to my cheeks, and I had to place a hand on one of them before I realized it was embarrassment.

"Why are you here?" I said, my eyes shifting around the room as I tried to plan an escape route.

"Grace called and told me she had a rough time bowling the other night. So I figured I'd sneak into her house and, you know, surprise her."

"So what are you doing in here?"

"Well, I didn't know where she was, and I didn't want to just wander around like a fool until I found her," Monroe said, giving me 'duh' eyes. "I was hoping someone, like *you* for instance, could tell me where she is so that I could just walk in all subtly."

I stared at Monroe and thought about the way he had burst into this room, and how each of his gestures seemed to be executed with one hundred percent of his effort. The combination of these observations made it hard for me to imagine that he could ever surprise everyone.

"Yes," I half-spoke, half-muttered to myself, "because you are truly the 'b' in subtle."

"So can you help me find her?" Monroe asked, giving me a look that he probably intended to be compelling.

"This place isn't that big!" I said, stretching my arms out. "You shouldn't need a map."

A huge grin erupted onto Monroe's face. "Actually, I do need a map."

"Why?" I said slowly, sensing a trap ahead.

"Because I keep getting lost in your eyes."

never trust a happy song

I narrowed my eyes at him. "Was that supposed to be a pick-up line?"

"Wow, you know what those are? Grace told me you were a brainiac at everything except how to be social." I felt my face twist. "Oh, was that insulting?" Monroe said, holding out his hands. "Crap, I'm sorry. I don't really have an inner filter. I say stupid stuff sometimes."

"Try all the time," a voice said, and I jerked around to find Grace standing in the doorway.

"True," Monroe said with a smile as he rushed over to give his friend a hug. "I was looking for you."

"I was in the bathroom," Grace said, her words muffled by his shoulder.

"Are you okay?"

Grace pushed him away. "Yes," she said, spreading out the word into multiple syllables. "Why wouldn't I be?"

They looked at each other for a moment before Monroe cracked a tiny smile and shook his head. "Okay, okay. So what are we doing next?"

Grace adopted what I guessed to be the thinker's pose, though her giggles made her body shake so much that it was hard to be sure. Monroe started laughing too when Grace lost her balance and tumbled onto the floor. "Ice cream?" Grace asked as she stood up and brushed off her overalls.

"Sounds good to me."

"You want to come, Cassidy?"

Although ice cream sounded really good, something about watching them interact made me not want to leave my room. I drew my legs up and wrapped my arms around them, feeling like a prickly cactus in this room full of bubbly giggles. "No thank you," I said.

Grace cocked her head, and I assumed she was contemplating whether to argue with me. "Well, okay," she said, although from her voice I could tell it was not. "We'll see you later."

"Okay."

Grace and Monroe left the room, both moving at the same bouncy pace. Her movements were graceful and his abrupt, but they still managed to walk in perfect harmony. I observed many distinctions between them, and yet couldn't help feeling that they were actually quite similar. Monroe was in all grey, yet I could imagine him wearing obnoxiously bright clothing and making the apparel seem completely normal. I could easily see Grace falling over laughing at one of Monroe's pick-up lines, and Monroe applauding Grace's gutter balls. These conclusions popped out of nowhere, with no real proof, but I believed them. The feeling was disarming, and made it difficult to resume working. This turned into annoyance as the thoughts continued. The image of Grace and Monroe together had replaced the image of Grace's sad face, and I couldn't let it go. And even worse, I now felt upset. I realized that I really, really wanted ice cream.

Oh, well. At least there's school tomorrow, I thought to myself, dropping back onto my bed with a sigh. *At least you have school.*

chapter 9

The bowling incident submerged itself in the icy pool of topics not to be mentioned. Grace never said as much, but I could tell. Every time I got even close to mentioning the word 'bowling', Grace would shrink away faster than if we were a pair of electrons. I wanted to discuss it with Likith, but again some instinct stopped me from mentioning it. Perhaps I was afraid that, if I did, Grace would eventually find out, which would then trigger a conversation I did not want to have. The worry was completely ridiculous, as Grace had never met Likith and did not have auditory superpowers, but it existed nonetheless. As I had no way of analyzing the mysterious incident, I tried to forget about it by burying myself in my ever-growing pile of work.

The rigor of Stanford's program picked up during the second week, as we began to study the relationship between math and science. Every day we watched lectures on the physics of a different property of the earth, eagerly waiting for the moment when we could delve into how to build machines that could then work in harmony with these properties. At least, that's how *I* felt. But I couldn't help thinking that everyone else felt the same. Some days I could feel our enthusiasm crackling through the air like electricity, as if the room was one big Van de Graaf generator. While in the lecture hall, I felt like I was on the same page as everyone around me. There were no joking innuendos or Grace giggles to get in the way. There, everything was in my language.

"Gravity affects every single thing on this earth," Mr. Deal said on Wednesday as he paced the lecture room's stage. "It affects everything from the turning of the planet to the ability of your organs to stay in your body. If the strength of gravity were greatly increased, your organs could be pulled right out of your body." The class collectively groaned at that thought, and Mr. Deal smiled. "Cool, right? Now, spend some time discussing the importance of gravity with your partner. If your partner is confused about anything, explain it to them." He stopped and stared at the class, as if expecting immediate results. Everyone stared back, and I wondered if he would realize that he had yet to tell us to start. Eventually, Mr. Deal sighed. "That means start talking now."

Likith immediately turned to me, and I suspected he had some little-known fact about the expulsion of organs up his sleeve. "Did you know that under very high G-forces, the pressure can cause our organs to explode?"

"That's absolutely revolting," I said, trying not to give him the satisfaction of seeing my face twist. I scanned my brain for an interesting fact to shoot back at him. "But not as disgusting as the Great Wall," I said, turning to face him. "Did you know that if someone died during construction, they would just build over them? That's messed up."

"Why? It's cheaper than bricks and it's not like they're running out of people."

"Likith!"

He chuckled. "What? Besides, that fact wasn't about physics."

never trust a happy song

"Of course it is! I was comparing the structural properties of the human body to that of bricks," I said, crossing my arms. Likith raised his eyebrows, and we stayed in this silent battle until I was unable to hold back a smile. "Okay, *fine*. So it wasn't my best. In my defense, physics isn't really my forte. I prefer history."

"Really?" Likith mulled this over for a second before saying, "Then why are you in a program for math and science?"

"My parents."

"Ah." He sighed, and I knew that he understood what I meant. For a split second, I considered asking him if he knew about John Brown. But then I realized that even if he had read the U.S. history textbook, he probably wouldn't remember a character that minor.

"All right, has everyone conversed?" Mr. Deal interjected into our silence. People around the room nodded, and Mr. Deal clapped his hands. "Good, then let's move on."

At the end of the lecture, Mr. Deal assigned a large packet of physics problems for homework. I cringed, remembering that I still needed to finish the math packet from Monday, which was due Friday. I calculated how much time I could spend on each packet and still get at least seven hours of sleep. For the last few nights, I had only been averaging five hours. My limbs were already beginning to wobble underneath my weight, due to lack of sleep.

When Mr. Harper's car pulled up to our lecture hall, I was surprised to see Grace's face through one of the windows. She hadn't come along to pick me up since last week, and in fact I'd barely seen her since Friday. To be honest, I'd rather enjoyed the break from her chatter. As I approached the car, I noticed that she seemed to be wearing the exact same overalls and pink rain boots as last week. I had originally assumed that that was her favorite outfit, but now I was wondering if it was some kind of uniform.

"How many pairs of overalls do you own?" I asked as I slid in next to her in the backseat.

"Well, hello to you too," Grace responded with a smile. Apparently, the dam separating us had collapsed, and Grace's normal enthusiasm was pouring out. I tried to smile back, but didn't really have the energy. "I have ten pairs," she eventually said with a giggle.

"Why?"

"I noticed that you wear them a lot, so I was wondering if it was the same pair or if you had duplicates."

"I have lots," Grace said, still smiling. "I love them. They are just so comfortable."

Grace stopped talking and began to hum. I used the break to contemplate this fashion choice, surveying the overalls again. They had wide straps that hung over her thin shoulders, and from there a mass of denim wrapped around her body and plunged downward to her feet. With the way she was sitting, the fabric pouffed outward so that she looked like a beach ball. Perhaps they were comfortable, but I couldn't imagine feeling secure with all that empty space inside my clothes. *They're definitely big*, I thought. *If we still had Prohibition, people would pay her to smuggle alcohol across the border in her overalls.*

"Do you have ten pairs of pink rain boots, too?" I asked.

never trust a *happy* song

Grace laughed loudly. "No, silly," she said, although I didn't feel silly. "I just have one. You don't get more than one pair of the same kind of shoes."

"Oh, yeah," I said, my voice faltering under the lie. "I knew that."

Grace smiled in response, and started to scuff her rain boots against the car floor. "Do you want to play a board game when we get home?" she asked eventually, each word emitted in harmony with a swing of her foot.

"Oh, well, I kind of need to work until dinner," I said, hoping desperately she'd just accept that and move on.

"Pshaw!" Grace said, flinging her hand through the air, as if to push away my wishful thinking. "Homework, schm-omework. I say you take a break and we play Sorry. Have you ever played Sorry? It's a lot of fun."

"Really, Grace," I pleaded. "I've got a lot to do and I'd really appreciate it if you didn't ask this of me right now."

"Please?" we both said at the same time. "Please?" she asked again, her eyes and mouth morphing into a pout. "It will be really fun."

Grace didn't seem to understand that 'fun' was an ineffective sales pitch. If she wanted me to do something with her on a weekday evening, she was going to have to offer more than a promise of fun and a cute pout. What I needed was a way to make my stress disappear. What I cared about was time. "Fine," I groaned. "But only for half an hour. I'm not going to play any longer than that."

"Yay!" Grace said as I slammed back into my seat, frustrated by my inability to say no to her puppy dog pout. I spent the rest of the ride contemplating this apparent weakness, and trying to ignore Mr. Harper's tiny smile, which was reflected in the rearview mirror.

Once we reached the house, it took Grace less than five minutes to find the board game. She set it up in my room, which made me uncomfortable, as I had no idea how long this game was going to last, and therefore had no idea how long it would be before I could get her out of there.

"All right, just think of this as school," Grace said as we sat down on the floor. "This right here is a lesson in the random properties of chance."

"I thought you didn't want me to connect fun activities to school," I said hesitantly, picking at a bit of carpet lint by my foot.

Grace looked serious for a single second, before her smile reemerged. "Well, I figured we have to start somewhere."

I wanted to ask 'Start what?', but the joy in Grace's smile made me swallow the question.

"So you have a piece and a home-base area," Grace said, her hands fluttering around the board. "And there are dice that you have to roll and cards to draw. The point of the game is to get all the way around the board and back to your home base before the other player does."

"That's it?" I asked, staring at the colorful array of squares and pathways before me.

"That's it," Grace said, flourishing her hand over the board one more time.

"Interesting."

never trust a *happy* song

Grace assigned me the yellow piece and gave herself the green. Then she rolled the die and began the game. The game was simple enough that after about three turns I was able to run through the motions on automatic.

"What do you want to be when you grow up? Like, what do you want to do?" Grace asked after five turns in silence. The question was so serious compared to the triviality of the game we were playing that it took a moment for me to realize that she'd really asked it. I recited my stock answer easily.

"I want to go to MIT and double-major in applied math and nuclear engineering," I said as I rolled a six and moved my piece across the board.

"Wow."

"What about you?"

Grace shrugged. "I don't know."

She said the words so simply that they seemed to float in the space above my head before solidifying and become real. My head shot up. "What? You have no idea?"

"I just finished my first year of high school," she said with a smile. "I don't really need to know yet."

I wanted to say "That's not true," but settled for the milder "Your school didn't coach you on how to pick your future classes and figure out what you want to study?"

Grace snorted. "No."

"Oh," I said, and looked down. The full monstrosity of the chasm of differences separating Grace and me was now knocking into my skull like a pendulum. The force of the realization shortened my breath, and I felt incredibly stupid sitting on the floor and moving plastic pieces around a plastic board. "Doesn't that scare you?" I had to ask.

"No. I know I'll figure it out. Maybe not in high school, but I'll figure it out eventually." Her casual tone was killing me, my lungs tightening as if all the oxygen was seeping out of the room. My heart beat faster as I felt the fear that she apparently didn't. "You look so horrified," Grace said, letting out a laugh that echoed around the room.

"But," I began, the volcano bubbling, "if you don't start now, you'll get behind and never catch up."

"Behind in what?" Grace asked, her smile thin and humoring.

My throat tightened, an innate reaction telling me that her smile needed to be wiped away before it was too late. "Behind in the competition. I know some people say that you don't need to start thinking about college until later, but they're wrong. It's like a ladder. If you don't maintain your footing and keep up the pace in high school, you won't be able to climb up to the best and therefore most desirable rung for college. And then you won't be able to continue up the ladder to the best grad school, and you'll never reach the top. If you fall off the ladder at the bottom, you can't just jump up to the top. And it won't be plausible for you to start up the ladder later on, because by then a new generation of climbers will have surfaced."

Grace showed no signs of stress. It didn't even seem like she was fighting off an onslaught of stress. I wondered what she knew that freshman Cassidy hadn't. "So you think we're in a race?" she asked, picking up her game piece and attempting to balance it on her nose.

never trust a happy song

"Yes!" I jumped at the word, pointing my finger right at the plastic figure. "It's a race. It's a slaughterhouse. It's millions of students trampling each other to make their way up a ladder that can only hold so many."

"What is it with you and this ladder?"

"*Grace*," I warned, gluing my eyes shut and gritting my teeth. I spoke slowly. "It's just a well-fitting metaphor, *okay*?"

I had shielded myself from Grace's smile, but I could still hear her giggles. She was laughing at me, like this was all some kind of a joke and the future wasn't going to come knocking on her door someday. I had always known that not every school was like mine, but the idea that there were actual *people* who went to those other schools was only now becoming real, as I saw the lack of fear and stress in Grace's face.

"Look, school is different for us," Grace said kindly, abandoning her game piece to twist a strand of her hair. "For you, school is this pathway to a future or whatever. For me, school is just ... school."

"Just school," I repeated, mimicking her tone. She nodded and I tried to stomach the idea. "I can't imagine that."

"I don't really enjoy school," Grace said with a shrug. "So I don't really do that well."

"Why?"

"Well, I'm kind of dumb."

"What?" I sputtered. "Don't say that!"

Grace let out her trademark giggle. "What? C'mon, you know you thought I was dumb when you met me." Grace looked at me in a

[71]

way that let me know she *knew* it was true, like in the way that I *knew* 1 + 1 = 2. Heat rushed to my face.

"Please don't say that," I said flatly. "It's bad. You need to believe in yourself."

Grace scoffed. "And who told you that, your school?"

"Well, yeah."

She pushed her lips into a smile, and without her teeth it looked almost sad. "My point exactly."

I wasn't able to speak, only stare at her. "So you really don't enjoy school?" I managed to squeak.

She was looking down at the game board, concentrating heavily on the movement of her game piece. "It's your turn," she said after a moment.

I nodded and rolled the dice, not wanting to push the question. "Do you know how long we've been playing?" I asked suddenly, the realization that I had no sense of what time it was exploding inside of me.

"Oh my stars," Grace muttered in response.

"You promised we'd only play for half an hour."

"I know. I haven't forgotten," Grace said, looking up at me through her eyelashes. "Just relax, Cassidy."

"I have to do my homework," I muttered, although I knew it wasn't going to do any good. Through my panic I heard the Mom voice: *Cassidy, you're not going to make it as a scientist if you can't learn from your mistakes. When a method fails, don't try it again.* I clenched my fingers into a fist to prevent myself from counting how many times I'd used the homework plea.

never trust a *happy* song

Grace sighed again, blowing her bangs upwards. "I can't imagine your life. Like, when do you have fun?"

"I don't," I said, and something about the words – something about the sudden truth in them – made me laugh. Grace joined in, laughing loudly, and it was possibly the first thing we had ever done in harmony. "At least," I amended, "not this kind of fun."

Grace continued to play the board game, and I went along with the motions. But now, instead of spacing out, I studied her face. When I had first met Grace, her whole appearance had seemed strange, and I realized now that it was because she was full of opposites. She wore baggy clothes, yet by looking at the way her neck curved down, I realized she was actually quite skinny. Her hair had seemed as bouncy and vivacious as the rest of her, but as I studied it now, I saw that each strand looked quite brittle. Her eyes were huge and yet, as she looked down at the board, they showed nothing but a tiny reflected image of our game. But what really set her apart from the people I knew back at home was her face. Her face was unlined, she had no heavy bags under her eyes, and her mouth wasn't closed in a taut line. She looked relaxed, even as she played this meaningless game. As we played, she began to hum the same six note tune that I had heard before, the song flowing out to paint the air with happiness.

"Grace," I blurted, "do those girls go to your school?" The question was out before I could stop it. Grace's head popped up and her hand froze mid-move.

"Yes," she said, resuming her movement. "They do. They're in my grade."

I nodded and took a deep breath, knowing that it was too late to back out now. "What do they mean when they say 'Grace the Disgrace'?"

Her hands froze again, only this time her eyes flicked up to bore right into mine. "I don't know," she said softly. "I guess they just don't like me." I nodded again and looked down, inarticulate. "But that's okay," she said, leaning down until she forced her eyes into my line of vision. "There are always going to be people who don't like you. Even in middle school there were people who thought I was weird, but I didn't let it bother me."

"Never?"

"Look, I know I'm kind of odd," Grace said. "I'm loud and I bounce around and I like to dress a certain way." Here she paused to crack a smile at me. "And I know that you don't really like me because of those things."

"No, no," I jumped in, feeling the heat return.

Grace waved her hand in front of my face. "Oh come on, you know it. I irritate you because I don't concentrate, just like you irritate me because you're working all the time. But, hey – we managed to sit down and play a board game without killing each other. I think that's saying something about the capacity of the human race to tolerate diversity." That made me laugh again, and the sound rang out in a way that I had considered unique to Grace. "You just have to find ways to have control and be okay with yourself."

I nodded and then stared forward, not knowing if I'd really gotten an answer to my question. "I think it's been half an hour," I said

never trust a happy song

as gently as possible, my hand groping the bed-side table behind me in search of a pencil.

"Okay," Grace said. "I won anyway."

"Congratulations," I said with a small smile, thinking that it was fitting for the one who actually enjoyed the game to be the victor.

"I'll get you when dinner is ready, all right?"

"All right."

I was worried that Grace was going to take her time in leaving. This seemed like something she'd enjoy: prancing around the room with the knowledge that every ticking second that I was unable to focus on my work was giving me more anxiety. But, for some reason, she must have decided to give me a back. Grace packed up the game and was out of the room in less than a minute.

chapter *10*

After Grace left my room, I tried to complete all of the assignments that were due the next day. However, my focus was so poor that I made embarrassing errors. At one point, I mistook Coloumb's Law for Newton's Law of Universal Gravitation, and I almost confused the speed of sound with the speed of light. $c = 3 \times 10^8$. *Or is it* 3.8×10^8...

I sat on my bed and let my pencil flounder across the page. With each mix-up, I felt my cheeks grow hotter. Images of Likith snickering as he watched me screw up kept popping into my head. I imagined him proudly pointing to his paper, where he no doubt had gotten every answer correct. Or maybe he wouldn't tease me, and instead would ask if I'd gotten enough sleep lately. Through my haze of exhaustion, I wasn't able to pinpoint which reaction would be his. My sense of reality was starting to blur with all of my personal nightmares. I got up and paced across the room. My sense of time numbed, and I'm not sure if I walked back and forth for minutes or hours. Eventually, Grace barged into my room, giggling that I was going to burn a hole through the floor and needed to come down for dinner.

The meal came and went in a blur, the Harpers' simple conversations about the summer heat and weekend golfing plans going in one ear and out the other.

"Cassidy," I heard at one point, and snapped back to the present.

"Yes?"

never trust a happy song

"You've hardly touched your food," Mrs. Harper said, looking at me with concerned eyes. "If you don't like it, don't be afraid to say so. I could easily get you something else."

"Oh, no, the food's fine," I said quickly, even though I hadn't even registered what was on my plate. "I'm just really stressed out about all the work I have to finish tonight."

"Oh?" Mrs. Harper asked, putting down her fork. "Do you need any help?"

"No, that's not it. I've been having trouble focusing."

"Oh, that's the worst," Mrs. Harper said, and I noticed that the pitch of her voice rose in direct proportion to her degree of sympathy. "You know, whenever I had trouble focusing in college I would always find a friend and talk it out. I found that after I had finished telling them what was on my mind, I was able to focus again. Maybe you could try that."

"Well, I guess," I said, although I knew my options for friends were slim, and I still didn't have Likith's phone number.

"I know!" Mrs. Harper exclaimed. "Why don't you call your mom?"

"Oh," I said, crumpling the edge of my napkin in my fist. I could feel each of the Harpers stare at me, as if waiting to see if I would give the correct response to Mrs. Harper's question. My mind raced, but I did not know what that answer could be. "I guess I could."

"Yes, why don't you do that right after dinner," Mrs. Harper said with a smile. "I bet you'll feel a lot better then." I tried to smile back, but something about the look on Grace's face told me it was fooling no one.

I walked very slowly to my room after dinner, thinking about what to say when my mom answered the phone. I still hadn't decided by the time I reached my room, and I hesitated to pull out my phone. But deep down, I knew that the mere fact it had been suggested to me meant that I'd have to do it. High school had instilled in me an inability to back down. *If I drop the class, it's on my permanent record. If I don't turn in the homework, my grade plummets. If I fail to make this call, I will forever remember the time that I was too afraid to call my mother.*

I only ever used my phone for calling Mom and asking fellow students homework questions. So it didn't take long for my reflexes to take over and bring up Mom's number. The next thing I knew she was saying hello – it was like the phone hadn't even rung at all.

"H-hi," I said, cursing myself for sounding so nervous.

"Cassidy!" Mom exclaimed. "Have you settled in?"

"Yes," I said. "How are you, Mom?"

"I'm good," she said, and hearing her voice made me realize that I missed her. Although hers did not offer the chipper and welcoming tone of Mrs. Harper's voice, her serious tone warmed me with its familiarity. "Busy, but good. I assume you're the same?"

"Well," I began, tracing the pattern of the carpet with my toes. "Actually I've been struggling a bit. Not grade-wise," I added quickly, not wanting to have to listen to her have a heart attack over the phone.

"With what, then?" Mom asked, switching to what I recognized as her 'Let's-get-down-to-business' voice.

"Establishing my routine, I guess," I said, picking my words carefully. "I haven't been concentrating as well."

"Are they distracting you?" she said, jumping in quickly. "Because I can get you another host fam–"

"No! It's not them," I said, even though I knew that it was. But the thought of leaving the Harpers didn't sit right with me now. I was too curious, too wrapped up in the differences between their lives and mine. Leaving now would be like returning the history book to the library before I'd found out who won the war.

"Well, what is it then, Cass?" my mom asked, calling me by the nickname she rarely used.

"I don't know. I ...." I faded off, wondering all of a sudden why I'd even called her. Then, it hit me. "Can you tell me again why you and Dad picked this program?" I asked. "Why was this the best choice?"

"Lots of reasons," Mom said, although she stopped there. I sat silently, determined not to back down just to avoid an awkward silence. Eventually she let out a big breath of air. "Well, for one, Stanford is a very good university, Cassidy. It's near the top of our list of options."

"I know that," I said. "I like Stanford a lot."

"Well, that's good. Second, it's good for you to get experience with academics outside of your high school environment. That way you'll be more prepared for what you will face in college."

"Right, I understand that," I said, pacing faster in an effort to will her to get to the point.

Mom paused for a second before continuing. "Third, Stanford is especially well known for its accomplishments in engineering research. You are in very good hands there, and having worked with their professors will look great on your application."

Bingo. "But why engineering?' I asked, and breathed in sharply as I waited for her response.

"What do you mean, why? We discussed this. Engineering is a useful and honorable profession, one that will get you a good job, and helps build a profile that colleges and grad schools like."

"But I don't even really like engineering," I said, crossing my fingers in hope that Mom wouldn't immediately shoot me down. "I'm good at the parts that involve mathematics, but then there's all this *science* .... Mom, you know that's not really my thing."

"I know you've struggled in that area in the past, but you've been improving." Mom sighed, a warning signal that her patience was running low. "Cassidy, what is this about?"

"I told you, I've been having problems concentrating. And I was thinking ... well, I was thinking that maybe the reason I'm having trouble is that engineering isn't for me. I've given it a lot of effort, but maybe it's time to try something new."

"And what would you do instead?"

"Well, my favorite subject is history."

"Cassidy, what jobs can you get as a history major?" Mom exclaimed, and I winced. "You can't be a teacher," she added, shooting down my next words before they were even out of my mouth. "That job won't support the lifestyle you deserve. Your father and I are trying to prepare you for a good life, Cassidy."

I swallowed, her words barreling into my ear like a bowling ball. I felt the *clunk* as they locked me into the gutter with the mention of "a good life." *What is a good life?* I wanted to ask, but I didn't. *I could be many other things besides an engineer and have a good life*, I wanted to say. *I could be a lawyer, or a business person,* I wanted to suggest. But I didn't.

Mom sighed, "Look, Cassidy. When it comes to your future, what matters is the school you get into and the career that you set yourself up for with that education. To be successful, you have to be practical and realistic. That means that favorites can't really be taken into account."

"Yes, Mom, I know that," I said, almost losing the battle to keep my volume down. I was mad at her, but I burned with embarrassment at the idea of Grace hearing me yell. She would no doubt bound into my room to see what was wrong, and then I would have to explain.

Mom was speaking very slowly and tersely now, like the calm before the explosion. "Then why are you asking?"

"I ... I don't know!" I yelled, with an odd laugh. I realized then how true that was. I had no idea why I was even bringing it up, because I had gone so far down the engineering path that it was probably too late for me to have any chance at change. Every argument I ever had with my parents ended with them winning, but the Harpers' optimism had fooled me into thinking that it might go my way this time. Instead of getting me anywhere, this argument had wasted precious time. "I should go finish my work," I said with a sigh.

"Yes, you should," Mom agreed. "But before you go, there's something I meant to tell you earlier. We received your score report from the SAT IIs you took in May."

"Oh?" My pulse rate shot up, and I tightened my grip on the phone. I analyzed the tone of Mom's voice, trying to infer from its pitch whether this was good or bad news.

"Yes!" Mom actually shouted, and then I knew that this was a rare moment of true excitement. "Cassidy, you got an 800 on both Math 2 and Chemistry!"

"Oh!" I attempted to say more, but my words disintegrated into excited squeals. The tension in my body changed from that of stress to excitement as my stomach filled with the incomparable feeling of victory. "I ... Are you serious?"

"Yes!"

"Oh, thank God!"

"You should be very proud, Cassidy."

"So, now I'm done!" I squealed, my euphoria rising at the thought. "I never have to take the SAT IIs again. I've crossed one more test off my list!" I felt even giddier at the thought of shortening the seemingly never-ending list of standardized tests required for college.

"Wait a minute, Cassidy," Mom said, and my heart almost stopped. "You need to take them again in the fall."

My happiness drained away, and I felt like I was going to puke. "Take them *again*? But ... I got 800s. I got *perfect scores*!"

"That is true."

"So why on *earth* would I take them again? That makes absolutely no sense, Mom!"

"Don't use that tone with me, Cassidy." Mom's voice dropped to the signature low tone that gave me nightmares when I was younger. "You took those tests when you were still a sophomore. Your father and I think you should take them again as a junior to prove to the colleges that you can really do it – to prove that it wasn't a fluke."

Her words sank in slowly, hitting me one by one. When I spoke again, I heard tears developing. "What do you mean, 'prove'? Why should I have to *prove* anything?"

Mom let out a big sigh, and I knew my question would not be answered. "Cassidy, I don't want to have this argument right now. You go do your homework, and let me worry about signing you up for the next test date."

"But–"

"I'll talk to you later, Cassidy," she said. I didn't attempt to continue. The conversation was over.

"All right, Mom," I said with a sigh. "Talk to you later."

My mom hung up first, and I stood there for a while with the phone to my ear, happy and angry and sad all at the same time. I wanted to jump up and down and squeal at my perfect 800s, and cry about the fact that I was going to have to retake the tests, and worry about the fact that I didn't really want to be an engineer. *Maybe they're right,* I thought. *Maybe I just need to try harder to like science.* I forced myself to believe that maybe it didn't matter whether my major was my favorite subject, as long as I could handle the work and be successful. And I would be able to handle engineering – that much I knew. I was always able to push myself that far.

I dropped onto my bed and returned to my homework, which was now a welcome respite from other unwelcome thoughts. As I numbed my worries, my mind began to work smoothly again. I lost track of time as I worked through sheet after sheet. It wasn't until I felt my head bounce off my collarbone and fly back up that I realized how exhausted I was. With much effort, I shifted my head to glance at my clock. Its glowing red numbers read 4:00 AM.

Time for bed, Cassidy, I said to myself, even though I still wasn't done with everything that was due tomorrow – make that today. *You need to go to sleep.* At some point during this internal tug of war my eyelids slowly drifted shut. I felt my body slump backwards onto the bed, and was enveloped in the seductive softness of my mattress.

chapter *11*

I felt like a zombie as I entered the lecture hall the next day. I surely looked like one too. I had slept right up to the minute before Mr. Harper said we needed to leave, didn't take a shower, and skipped breakfast. The world was too bright and my stomach was screaming at me. The walls of the lecture hall waved gently back and forth and the professor's slides blurred before my eyes. Likith asked me several times if I was all right, saying that my head had been periodically sinking downwards.

"It's like you're a human yo-yo," he explained, "but the only part of your body experiencing the effects of gravity is your head."

"Ugh, please don't talk about physics," I groaned, bringing my hand up to my ringing head. "I don't even want to think about that."

"Well, you're in luck," he said. "Our next class is on writing. Apparently we're being assigned some giant research paper."

"Oh, joy," I exclaimed, glaring at Likith.

"Hey, I'm just the messenger," he said, shielding his face with his hands. Then he folded them under his chin and stared straight at me. "Maybe in the future you should get more sleep," he said softly. "Or at least drink more coffee."

"The coffee sounds more plausible," I said, silently praying that the Harpers had a coffee maker.

At that moment, Professor Morris bounded onto the lecture hall stage. "Good morning," he boomed, even though it was after lunch. "I hope you are having a good day."

Although I can function on almost no sleep, my perception of what people are saying sometimes gets a little fuzzy. Time seemed to move in fast-forward as I spaced out for entire chunks of Mr. Morris's lecture. Likith occasionally flicked me on the arm and asked if I was okay.

"Mr. Morris is talking about the essay now," he whispered at one point. "You really need to listen."

I opened my eyes as wide as I could and focused all my energy on the man at the front of the room. "You will write a fifteen to twenty page paper for your midterm project," he said, each word a sonic boom in my ears. "Your paper is due on July twentieth. Students in end seats, please take a rubric and then pass the stack down your row," he said. Papers rustled as we complied, while Mr. Morris briskly paced the stage. "As explained in the instructions given in your rubric, your paper must be a carefully researched study of how the laws of physics affect a particular object in the world."

"Physics," I groaned to Likith. "Great."

"Hey, it's not that bad," he whispered back. "You could focus more on the object than its physical properties. In fact, instead of an object, you could do a person!" Likith began to snicker lightly. "You could even write about Grace. Who I think it would be really interesting to meet, by the way."

I glared at Likith. "I am not going to write about Grace. There'd be no way to have any sources for the research. Besides, that's called stalking," I hissed.

"Whoa there, I was just joking," Likith whispered with a smirk. I stuck my tongue out at him before focusing back on Mr. Morris.

never trust a happy song

"Also," Mr. Morris said as he projected a slide entitled "Stanford Summer Program Social". "We will hold a social event this Friday night, June twenty-sixth. All students and host families are invited to join us for an evening of refreshments and good conversation. We will also honor a few students who have done an exceptional job with their coursework this summer." Mr. Morris spoke like the event would include the announcement of a ground-breaking new scientific discovery. To me it just sounded like a night of having to recite your plans for the future over and over again.

"Will you be going to that?" I whispered to Likith.

"Only if you come and bring Grace," he whispered back with a grin.

"Why do you want to meet her so badly?" I said, annoyed at his persistence.

"That girl not only irritates you, but makes you doubt the legitimacy of your approach to life," Likith said, emphasizing his key points with a firm nod of his head. "Oh, I must meet her."

"Fine," I said. "Be prepared for lots of small talk."

"Oh, I have so much small talk up my sleeve," he said with a mischievous grin. "You don't even know the half of it."

"That doesn't mean you can recite your nerdy pick-up lines to her all night."

"But I want to see if she understands them!" Likith whined, his voice jumping in pitch.

"She's not dumb," I hissed. The words seemed to boomerang through the air, and only once they returned to me did their meaning sink in. "She's just not like us. Now listen to the teacher!"

[*87*]

"We'll send invitations to your host families," Mr. Morris continued, "and we would like all of you to attend. Plus, we wouldn't want one of the students that we're honoring to not be there." Mr. Morris winked at us, and I realized that the awards were the teachers' form of bribery to get the students to socialize with adults. And it was working, because I had to admit that the idea of having a certificate of merit to show to my parents was enough to make me excited to go.

"I foresee a night of pointless conversation over hors d'oeuvres," Likith whispered to me, "time that would be better spent working on our research paper."

That sounded so freakishly like my mother that for a second I thought she had materialized beside me. "That's probably true," I said once the sensation of her presence had slid away, "but we could use the time out of the house." Likith gave me a sideways glance and I realized he had no doubt been parroting his own parents. "You know it's true."

"Yes," he said. "But my parents would definitely believe the opposite."

"Same here," I sighed, propping my head up with my hand. "Ugh, I am so tired."

"That's because you got like three hours of sleep last night."

"But I do that at least twice a week at home!" I exclaimed, hating the slight shake of my arm underneath the weight of my head.

"Well, this isn't home. This is a different environment, so you're probably getting even more stressed out here, which is making your body more tired." After Likith finished, he crossed his arms as if showcasing the results of his brilliant analysis.

"That was a very logical observation," I said for his benefit, clapping my hands together slowly.

"Shut up," Likith said, pushing me away. "Just get some sleep."

"Yes, sir!"

When I entered the house after the drive back from Stanford, I found Mrs. Harper, Grace, and Monroe already seated at the dinner table.

"Early dinner today," Mr. Harper said as he took off his shoes, oblivious to the shock on my face. I did not feel at all prepared to face the full cast of characters. Alone, they were headaches, but together they were sure to create a migraine-worthy extravaganza of small talk and humorous comments.

"Hi," Monroe said, waving cheerfully at me from across the table.

"Um, hi," I said, not sure how to react to his hospitality. "Is there a special occasion?" I asked, sitting down at the table.

"Nope," Grace responded. "Monroe was hanging out here and decided to stay for dinner."

"I didn't just *decide*," Monroe said with a scoff. "Geez Grace, that paints me in such an unflattering light. I received an offer I could not refuse."

"Okay, Monroe," Grace said, laughing. "Whatever you say."

"No arguing at the dinner table," Mr. Harper said with a smile. Then he turned to me. "While I was waiting for you to finish school today, the program coordinator told me that the camp is holding a social night."

"Yes, they are," I said once my mouth was free. "Although I'm pretty sure the focus of the night is going to be the awards."

Mr. Harper stopped mid-chew. "Awards?"

"Yes. They'll present awards to students who've done particularly well so far."

"Oh, then we must go!" Grace chirped, clapping her hands together. "Cassidy's sure to get one of those awards. After all, she's been working so hard." Grace's face betrayed nothing, and yet I suspected that her comment indicated just how annoying she found my work habits. I tried to find the words to explain that hard work alone wasn't enough to merit a prize, but the look on Grace's face told me that she wouldn't understand.

"I do think it would be a good idea to go," Mrs. Harper said, and she and Mr. Harper exchanged a nod. "Cassidy's been very diligent, especially considering the fact that it's summer vacation." Mrs. Harper smiled at me then, and I felt my cheeks grow warm.

"Well, it's set then!" Grace said, practically bouncing in her chair. Then she turned to Monroe, who had been the only silent one during the conversation. "I know you're feeling awkward, Monroe, so we might as well invite you too."

"Grace!" Mr. Harper scolded. "This is Cassidy's night. It's her decision who to invite."

Grace rolled her eyes and turned to me. "Cassidy, would you be okay with Monroe coming too?"

I managed to summon a shrug, overwhelmed by all the back and forth. I had never seen so much importance given to one night of academic awards. To my parents, awards were a necessary part of doing well, a normal happening. But at this moment, the idea of being honored felt extremely special. I forgot my exhaustion as a small smile crept across my face.

"Looks like she doesn't mind," Grace said, giving her dad a smile.

"All right," Mr. Harper said cheerfully. "Monroe's like family anyway. Goodness knows he's over here enough."

"Except when my dad is making me study," Monroe chimed in. Then he smiled and turned to Grace, "Which reminds me. We still need to have a bowling session to make up for the last one."

"Yes!" Grace exclaimed, fist bumping Monroe. "An epic adventure of neon spandex and gutter balls." As Grace squealed, I crossed my fingers under the table, praying that Monroe constituted sufficient companionship. "Cassidy, would you come too?" she asked, pulling the rug out from under my feet.

"Oh, um," I muttered, trying to remember the polite way to say no.

"Please," Grace whined.

"I don't know … I–"

"Come on," she coaxed, leaning forward. "You know you want to."

"Well, actually I don't."

Grace pointed a finger at me. "You do. I know you do."

I couldn't tell whether she was trying to be funny or irritating, but my annoyance was mounting nonetheless. "Grace, I just said that I don't want to," I said, slowing my pace in an effort to push the words into her skull. "I'm pretty sure that I know how I feel."

"Oh my stars!" Grace exclaimed. Then she whispered to Monroe, "Don't worry, we'll get her. She actually wants to go. She's just playing hard to get." My hand clenched. It was a small thing, so insignificant that I normally would have been able to overlook it. But it had been a long day and my patience level had hit zero.

"Grace!" I snapped, feeling tears in the corners of my eyes. "This is not funny. I absolutely *do not* want to go bowling!"

The room became silent. It was as if everyone was afraid to move, in case that might accidentally set off the next dreadful outburst. I was equally still, until I realized that I was holding my breath. My stomach contracted and a shaky breath exploded from my mouth. *Breathe Cassidy*, I commanded. *Just breathe.*

"Cassidy," Mrs. Harper asked cautiously. "Are … are you okay?" Her hesitation was a blemish in her usually fluid voice. I looked up to see the worry on her face and started to cry in earnest, my cheeks becoming stained.

Come on, get yourself together. Think calming thoughts. John Brown so desperately wanted to end slavery that he condoned the use of violence. If you square an even number, the result will always be even. The speed of a rollercoaster can be determined by its change in height. Sacagawea broke down language barriers to join Lewis and Clark on their expedition. Get yourself together.

"I'm sorry," I said after a few failed attempts to speak. "I'm sorry, I'm just so tired. I don't know why I'm crying, I really don't."

Mrs. Harper continued to look alarmed and I just wanted to make the tears stop. Poor Mrs. Harper – she hadn't bargained on this. She had probably thought that taking in a student for the summer would be fun, not knowing that such a mess would come with it. *Pull yourself together.*

"You don't have to go bowling," Grace said after a few more sobs, and I looked up to see that she too looked scared. I felt so relieved that she was scared instead of hurt that a sob got caught in my throat and I began to cough. I ducked my head down, using the crook of my arm to cover my coughs, when I felt two arms encircle me. I felt denim against the back of my neck, and knew then that it was Grace.

"I think you need to go to bed," I heard her say.

It sounded so nice, and I was consumed with imagining the feeling of a soft bed cradling my limbs. But then another thought hit and panic flooded through me. "But I have so much homework to finish."

"You can finish it later," Grace said, her tone making it very clear that there was no room for negotiation.

"But–"

"Look at me," she said, and I slowly tilted my head back to look up at her face. "The world will not end if you finish your homework later."

The words actually made sense, and I felt the last bit of resistance drain from my body. "Okay."

Then everything became fuzzy. I think Mr. Harper carried me upstairs and Grace tucked me into bed. Or it might've been Monroe, or maybe even Mom. The next thing I knew I was lying in a dark room on something soft, unable to do more than fall asleep.

chapter *12*

After my meltdown at the dinner table, Mr. and Mrs. Harper tiptoed around me as though the slightest touch would dissolve the nuclear attraction of my atoms. Grace, however, had almost the opposite reaction, and glued herself to my side. Unless she was at diving practice or I was at school, we were hydrogen and oxygen. At first I felt guilty about how her presence irritated me, but then I decided that if she was going to insist on togetherness, she would have to tolerate my pendulum-like emotions.

The day before the Stanford social, Grace insisted that we go to the mall to buy a dress that I could wear for the occasion. I thought that it was hypocritical for a girl clad in overalls and rain boots to be pushing fashion. But then I realized that I had been wearing the same pair of jeans for three days, so I was in no position to judge her.

"Do it," she said as we sat at a table by the edge of the mall. We had already found a dress, and were now seeking solace from the bright sun under the table's umbrella.

"No."

"Come on," she said, poking the inside of my arm. "Do it!"

"Ugh, fine." I gave Grace a final glare before rising from my chair, clearing my throat, and tapping the shoulder of the girl at the adjacent table. "Um, excuse me?"

The girl whipped her head around, and her long hair flew out in a fantastic blond web. "Yes?" she asked.

"I just wanted to say that I think the bow in your hair is really pretty."

never trust a *happy* song

She blinked a few times before responding. "Thanks."

I nodded, not knowing what else to say. When I dropped back into my chair, I was confronted by a smirking Grace.

"There you go! Was that so hard?"

"Yes," I grumbled, covering my face with my hands.

"No, it wasn't," Grace said, and I could hear her smile.

"I feel stupid," I said, bringing my head back up. "Could you tell me what the point of that was?"

Grace gave me a look, as though it should be obvious. "You basically just said it yourself. You shouldn't feel stupid doing things like that. It's important to be able to say something nice to a stranger. You know, seize the day and all that." Grace looked over at the girl with the pretty bow, who had gone back to sipping her latte. She did it daintily, as if her only focus for the entire day was the consumption of her foamy beverage. My hands clenched the edge of the table as I wondered if I'd ever be able to drink something as if I had all the time in the world. "And it totally worked," Grace continued, my attention snapping back to her. "Did you see how happy she looked after you said that?"

I frowned, thinking back to the alarmed look on the girl's face when I had tapped her shoulder. She had looked like how I felt whenever Grace barged in on me while I was working. That's probably how she would remember me: the latte-break interrupter. "Did you see how annoyed she looked before I said that?"

"She even thanked you!" Grace exclaimed. "She totally appreciated it."

"Saying thanks does not mean that you appreciate something."

Grace rolled her eyes and blew her bangs up so that they formed a spiky design on her forehead. "Fine. Don't believe me. That doesn't change the fact that you just seized the day!"

"Seized the day?" I repeated, wincing at the phrase. "Seriously, Grace? I think 'seize the day' is meant to describe something a little more momentous than complimenting someone's bow."

"Baby steps, my friend," Grace said, dismissing my comment with a flick of her hand. "Right now it's a compliment. Soon enough you'll be doing things like skipping for no reason, and then eventually ...," here Grace paused to do a little drum roll on the table, "wearing neon clothing to a bowling alley!"

I recognized then that I had fallen into a trap. Grace was trying to *teach* me to be more like her. I couldn't decide whether to be disgusted or proud of her planning skills.

"Very clever, Grace," I said, shaking my head slightly. "Can we go home now? I have an assignment to finish."

Grace frowned. "We're going to have to work on that. You need to be able to be out and about without thinking of everything you still have to do for school."

"Stop trying to condition me, Grace," I said. "You're making me feel like one of Skinner's monkeys."

Grace tilted her head. "Who's Skinner?"

"Haven't you heard of radical behaviorism?"

"No."

"Then never mind," I said with a sigh, thinking that Grace's lack of knowledge was something *I* needed to work on.

"Now let's go."

never trust a happy song

"Fine, you spoilsport," Grace said, grabbing my shopping bag and swinging it over her shoulder.

"Actually," I added, catching sight of a hamburger shop across the way. "Can we get some food first? I just realized I'm starving."

Grace followed my gaze to the hamburger shop, and stared at it for a second. "Sure," she said eventually. Then a devilish smile spread across her face. "But only if you skip on the way there."

"Ugh, seriously?" I said with a groan. "I don't have time to deal with this, Grace. I just want to get some food and then go back to work."

"Then the sooner you start skipping, the sooner you'll be back at work," Grace sang, twirling a piece of her hair.

"Why can't we just walk?" I desperately searched for logic to prove my point. "Walking is so much more efficient than skipping. Skipping is mostly upward velocity, which is pointless when you're trying to go forward."

"Who cares about efficiency!" Grace said, placing her hands on my shoulders and giving me a shake. "It's *fun*."

"No."

"Please," she said, dragging out the word like a little kid.

"I said, no!"

Grace opened her mouth as if to beg again, but then I saw her eyes light up. "If you don't skip, I'll say 'Oh my stars' over and over again for the whole drive home."

I felt my mouth drop open. "You wouldn't."

"Oh, I would."

Almost a minute passed before I was able to pull my mouth shut. For a moment, Grace looked more conniving than I could have ever imagined. "Ugh, fine," I said, pursing my lips together. "Let's skip."

"Yay!" Grace exclaimed as she linked her arm through mine and began propelling us forward. I stared at her smiling face as we jumped into the air, knowing that mine wore a scowl. We made it halfway to the shop before a voice rang out across the parking lot, whereupon Grace stopped mid-skip.

"Nice skipping, Grace," the voice said. "What are we, in the fifth grade?"

Grace let go of my arm, and the sudden lack of guidance made me stumble. As my balance faltered, I smacked right into a girl who had been standing to our left.

"Oh, I'm sorry," I said, immediately backing away.

The girl brushed off her shirt and grunted slightly. "Whatever." Then her eyes moved to Grace. "Grace the Disgrace!" she drawled, popping her hip out. I stared at the girl, my eyes flashing with recognition at the nickname. *How can there be so many of them?* "What are you doing at a shopping mall?" she said. "I mean, it's obvious you don't actually buy clothes."

Grace's face crumpled before she resumed her usual pleasant smile. "I was helping my friend buy a dress."

"Your friend," Mean Girl repeated, turning to study me. Her mouth morphed into a smirk, no doubt intended to be condescending. "Did you have to pay her or something?"

I frowned, not understanding her logic. "What are you talk–," I began, but then I caught Grace's gaze and stopped. Her eyes were huge, like a gazelle caught in a lion's trajectory. I was Sacagawea, looking out over a treacherous river covered in thin ice.

"No, I didn't have to pay her," Grace said, and I was alarmed by how shaky she sounded. "And anyways, why do you care?"

Mean Girl continued to smirk at me, and now I was the helpless victim. "I just feel sorry for this poor girl." She tilted her head, as if needing to view me from a different angle. "Do you understand that by being friends with Grace the Disgrace, you're basically committing social suicide?"

Grace stuttered slightly. "Please–"

"That's not possible," I blurted, unable to hold my tongue any longer.

"Excuse me?" Mean Girl said, switching hips.

"Suicide can only be committed by a living being. 'Social' is an adjective, a non-living descriptor, and therefore can't commit suicide."

"Oh my God," the girl said after a moment. "You're just as much of a freak as she is." She moved her head back and forth, her gaze of horror split between us. "I'm out of here," she said after a moment, her horror morphing into disgust. "See you later, Grace the Disgrace." Mean Girl turned on her heel and stalked off, leaving Grace and me in uncomfortable silence.

"I'm going to get us some burgers," I said eventually, struggling to stay afloat in the midst of Grace's watery eyes.

"I don't want one," Grace said very quietly. "You go, and I'll call my dad to come pick us up."

"Aren't you hungry?" I asked. Grace had gotten permission to have us shop straight through dinnertime, so it was now an hour past when we would normally eat.

"No," she said, shaking her head. "I'm fine."

"Are you?" I asked, reaching my hand out. It hung there awkwardly in the air, too unsure to advance further and touch her shoulder.

"Really. I'm not hungry," Grace said, wrapping her arms around herself. Then she let out an unnecessary laugh. "Geez, you're acting like my mom."

"All right, if you're sure." I began to walk towards the burger shop, but then stopped as a thought dawned on me. "Grace," I said, turning back, "that girl seems kind of dumb." Grace looked at me for a moment, and I wondered if she had heard me at all. "I mean, it seems to me that she actually takes pride in acting extremely dumb."

"Don't say that word," Grace said eventually, her voice too quiet. "It's not a nice way to describe someone."

"But she is," I blurted, stopping myself just before I said the apparently forbidden word. "And you're not," I said slowly. "I know you're not."

"Okay," Grace said. I nodded and then turned toward dinner, wondering if I looked as awkward as I felt. "Thanks." I paused and glanced over my shoulder to see Grace smile slightly, although I thought I also saw the track of a tear. I smiled back, and then continued to walk away. My feet moved forward, but my head was back with a wilted Grace, replaying the confrontation in a desperate attempt to understand it.

chapter *13*

    I struggled to understand how Grace could instantaneously switch from being incredibly loud and bright to worryingly quiet. I had seen it happen at the bowling alley and then again at the mall. It seemed like the Mean Girls had found her secret on/off switch, and found joy in flipping it back and forth. I pictured the schematic of the Circuit of Grace in my head: her wires coursing with joy, and each Mean Girl a resistor. *A circuit's flow of charge can be slowed or disrupted by a device called a resistor. The flow can be completely stopped by the opening of a switch, which then breaks the circuit.* The Mean Girls' resistance threatened Grace's flow of energy, first stopping her giggles, then her humming, then her smile. Eventually they would have nothing left to do but open the switch. I could easily imagining that happening; it almost seemed inevitable.

    There was something else, however, that made even less sense. As baffling as Grace was, at least she had consistently been a mystery to me. But now I felt an influx of worry and concern for the girl. I couldn't stand her at times, and yet I also cared. Even more baffling was that the caring had overtaken me with no warning. As I watched Grace limply emerge from the car post-mall and start towards the house, I tried to pinpoint the day that I had started caring about her. But I couldn't. No observable symptoms or established precedent had hinted that I was vulnerable to this caring. It just happened.

    About ten minutes after we arrived, Monroe appeared at the front door. Grace must have called him, because I saw the worry lines on his face. I let him in and returned to the bottom step of the staircase, where

I had been sitting with my legs pulled up to my chest, trying to analyze what had happened. Monroe sat down beside me, sprawling his legs out over the floor.

"Do you know them?" I asked, not looking at him. My face was pressed into the wood supports of the railing, my thoughts still dedicated to wringing meaning from the events of the day.

My question must have startled Monroe, because he took a while to answer. "Who?"

"Those girls," I said. I wanted to say more, but my mouth felt too dry. I hoped that he would just know what I meant.

"Not really," Monroe finally answered. Then, "I know she used to be friends with them, though."

I snapped my head up to look straight at him. "What?"

"She used to be friends with them."

I thought about that for a second, trying to imagine Grace arm-in-arm with a beautifully dressed, make-up encrusted girl who would clearly never skip. "No way."

"It's true."

"That's impossible," I said as I briskly shook my head. "I don't believe it."

Monroe shrugged. "Whatever, you don't have to. But it's true."

We were silent for a long time then, both of us sitting hunched over on the stairs. "How?" I finally asked, having identified no plausible circumstances under which Grace and the Mean Girls could have been friends.

I was looking forward again, but out of the corner of my eye I saw Monroe bring his legs up and run both his hands through his hair. "I'm not completely sure. I didn't really know her back then."

"Oh."

"But I'm guessing they were friends, and then things just changed."

His words were not enough, just a vague hint that made me want to know more. "What changed?"

Monroe turned to look at me, and suddenly all the humor was back in his face. "The people. They changed." I stared at him, unblinking, and he began to laugh. "Geez, people *do* change, you know."

"I guess," I said. Then I was silent, thinking about how much changing would have to happen for Grace and the Mean Girls to ever be alike. *A lot of changes*, I decided. A lot of changes must have happened between then and now. But 'a lot' wasn't specific enough – I craved a more precise quantity. I wanted clarity and precision.

"Boy, do I hate awkward silences," Monroe muttered. "They make reaching for a girl's hand so much more noticeable." I was familiar with Monroe's devotion to humorous commentary, but I still felt my cheeks begin to blaze. I pressed my head into my hands, embarrassed that I had drifted off into silence.

From my cave of embarrassment, I heard Monroe laughing. "Geez, Cassidy, I was just trying to lighten the mood." Then he jumped up from the stairs, spinning to look at me. "So, are we just going to sit here like two potatoes on a couch, or go talk to Grace?"

I clasped my legs, feeling the power of his scrutiny. "I hadn't realized there was a 'we.'"

Monroe laughed. "Well, come on, you're Grace's friend now too. I think that should've been evident by the number of times she's tried to get you to do stuff with us."

"I hadn't realized that equated to friendship," I said quietly.

Now Monroe laughed louder. "Good God, Cassidy. Do you really think Grace is going to ask someone she doesn't consider her friend to go bowling with her? The bowling alley is her special place that she's oddly and kind of creepily attached to. It's just like those refrigerator magnets. She is so obsessed with those things." Monroe rolled his eyes and nudged my shoulder as he spoke, as if I was supposed to share his bafflement at Grace's obsessions. But even though I did, I wasn't sure how I should react.

"I don't know," I said slowly.

Monroe leaned closer to me, his mouth turned up in what resembled a smirk. "I hope you realize I could be playing video games right now. But no, I left Princess Peach stranded in a tower to race over here."

"All right!" I said, intensely uncomfortable with his closeness. "All right, just move a little bit that way." I waved an arm in the opposite direction, and Monroe smiled.

"Finally," he said. "I thought I was never going to get a laugh out of you."

Only then did I realize I was giggling. The light, bouncy quality of the sounds reminded me of Grace. "Okay, I want to talk to her first."

Monroe raised an eyebrow. "You sure?"

"Yes," I said, hoping that if I said the word confident, believe the lie. Then I stood up and, realizing I had no idea ...re she was, began to pace the hallway.

"Calm down, Nancy Drew," Monroe said after I had crossed the space four times. "I can absolutely guarantee that she's in the kitchen."

I glared at him before directing my steps swiftly towards the kitchen. Sure enough, Grace was there, sitting cross-legged on the floor in front of the refrigerator. She was, I observed, in the exact same position she had been the first time I'd seen her playing with magnets.

"What are you doing?" I asked, the words flying out of my mouth before I could think of a more sensible question.

"Life is full of music," Grace read to me proudly. I dropped to the floor next to her, and she gave me a small smile. "That's the sentence I just made. See?"

I did see, and I watched as Grace traced the line of magnets with her finger. Her touch seemed so gentle, as if the words on the magnets could be erased by the pressure of her fingertip. "Grace," I found myself saying. "They're just magnets."

I saw Grace's throat move as she swallowed, and wanted to punch myself for talking. "Just because they look like magnets, doesn't mean that's all that they are."

"I'm sorry, I just ...." I stared straight at the magnets, hoping that they would magically form a new sentence and tell me what to say. "It would drive me crazy. Sitting here, doing nothing. I can't imagine how you do it."

I watched nervously as Grace reached up and began to twirl a lock of her hair. As I followed her movements, I became aware of how thin her hair actually was. "It makes me feel better," Grace said softly.

"Well, that's good, because I know I'm sucking at it."

"Yep," Grace said with a nod, and something about her wry smile made me giggle. "I guess they don't teach a class in empathy at that smart school of yours."

We fell into a comfortable silence, and although part of me would have been perfectly happy to sit there in silence forever, the other logic-obsessed part of me just wouldn't shut up. "So, when you want to feel better, you sit here and play with magnets?" I asked.

"Yep."

"Why?"

Grace rolled her eyes and blew a puff of air up into her bangs. "Why not?"

"Well, because it's not giving you anything useful," I said, still staring at the mysterious magnets. "There's no purpose."

"There is *so* a purpose!" Grace exclaimed, swinging her legs around so that she was now facing me.

"What?"

"It's giving me joy."

Many potential responses flooded into my head: how can the magnets trigger an emotional response? Why do you feel so attached to them? Is there a fundamental force of attraction that I didn't learn about in chemistry class? But instead of asking any of those things, I just said, "Okay."

never trust a *happy* song

Grace's face lit up, and it was as if the encounter at the mall had never happened. "Okay, time for another lesson."

"Oh, no."

"Yes!" Grace squealed, pulling at my sleeve. "I want you to close your eyes and listen."

"Okay," I said wearily, closing my eyes. Then, realizing that I had no context for the assignment, "Listen for what?"

"The music."

I tried to connect the dots, but my mind came up blank. "I'm sorry?"

"Remember," Grace sang, "life is full of music."

I wanted to tell her that was ridiculous. I wanted to explain to her that I couldn't hear music when no one was playing music – that musical notes weren't like the laws of physics, and they didn't exist as invisible parameters of the world. But before I could form the words, I remembered that I was trying to make her feel better. I was trying to undo what the Mean Girls had done and flip her switch back into its normal position.

"Okay," I said tentatively. Then I tried. I tried for what felt like an hour. But I couldn't hear anything. "Grace, I feel stupid."

"Shh!"

"Grace, there isn't even anything for me to be–"

"Cassidy. Just. Listen."

"To what?"

"I told you," Grace said, opening her eyes to glare at me. "The music!"

My Grace-tolerance quota for the day had been reached, and thoughts of all the homework I had yet to finish rushed in. "I don't hear anything," I said irritably.

"Well then, you're not listening hard enough!" Grace yelled.

"This is *stupid*!" I yelled, our volumes now matching. "I come in here, and I try to talk to you because for some reason *I* feel bad...." As I trailed off, I saw Grace flinch, and my anger levels fell. "I'm going to get Monroe," I said, soft once again. "He would be much better at this."

"Yes," Grace said, as I stood up. "Go back to your textbooks and your A-plus essays and never-ending knowledge so that you no longer have to deal with annoying dumb people like *me*!"

I froze, and my heart launched itself in fury at my brain. "Grace."

When I mustered the courage to turn around, I saw that Grace was standing up, her hand braced against the refrigerator. "I'm sorry," she said, her eyes very large and glossy. "That was out of line."

I tilted my head down, not wanting to get caught up in trying to identify all the emotions in Grace's eyes. In my peripheral vision, I saw Monroe standing in the entrance to the dining room, his frame very tense. "It's okay," I said eventually, unsure if it really was, but unable to think of anything more appropriate. I was turning away, ready to bury myself in a big textbook, when Grace spoke again.

"And thanks, Cassidy, for all the help. You must think I'm pathetic, getting so upset."

"No, I understand," I said, still looking away. "Those girls seem, you know ...."

Grace's eyes twinkled, as if she was inwardly laughing at my cowardice. "What?"

never trust a *happy* song

I sighed, clenching my fists in preparation to hit the bulls-eye. "They seem so mean."

"Yeah," Grace said with a laugh. "They sure are." And suddenly that's all she was doing – just laughing. Her frame shook with her trademark bell-like giggles, and I ran down the hallway, catching a glimpse of the worry on Monroe's face before I escaped up the stairs.

chapter *14*

To me, the Friday of the social seemed like any other day. But Mrs. Harper treated it like a holiday, making an extra big breakfast and telling me that I should feel proud to be taking classes at such a great institution. I told her it was hard to feel proud when this kind of thing was just expected of me, and she frowned.

"You should feel proud," she said, placing her hand on the back of my chair. "The mere fact that you were accepted into the program means that someone there thinks highly of you. It means they believe you will do important things during your life, and be a significant contributor to the world."

It was a nice thought, but unfortunately not necessarily true. Acceptance meant potential, not success. "To be seen as significant in the eyes of others," I repeated, mulling over the phrase as I chewed on a piece of bacon. "It's a nice thought, Mrs. Harper. But I doubt it's inevitable. There are way too many people in this world. Too much competition."

"Life doesn't have to be a competition," Mrs. Harper said, and I imagined the horrified look that would have crossed Mom's face if she was here. I looked up to see that Mrs. Harper was staring at me, her eyebrows knitted together. "You know, you worry me sometimes, Cassidy." I didn't know what to say to that, so I just thanked her for the good breakfast and left to get ready for school.

The day became even odder when I came home from school to find Grace and Monroe sitting on my bed, playing a card game.

"Guys," I whined, throwing my backpack to the ground. "One, this is my room. Two, you know that I sit on the bed while I work."

"Oh no," Grace said, not taking her eyes off her cards. "You're not doing any work today. Today's Friday. Friday is fun day."

"Says who?" I said, placing my hands on my hips.

"Says me. Plus, the social starts in a few hours. We'll have to start getting ready at some point, so we should have fun until then."

"Whoa, whoa, whoa," Monroe said, dropping his cards so that they scattered all over the bed. "When you invited me over you said nothing about getting ready. I do not want to be stuck in some kind of makeup-crazed does-this-dress-make-me-look-fat fest. You know I'm not good in situations like that."

"Calm down, Monroe," Grace said. "Does it look like either of us are big makeup people? We'll probably start getting ready in like two hours."

"Phew," Monroe said, wiping his forehead with his hand. "Disaster averted." Then he turned to me. "So, Cassidy, you up for a game of Go Fish? Don't be thrown off by the name," he said, no doubt seeing the less than thrilled look on my face. "It's a very serious and philosophical game. We're contemplating life here."

"Uh ...." I trailed off, and wished Grace could give me a lesson in how to navigate Monroe's humor. "Sure. How do you play?"

Monroe gawked at me. "How do you play? It's Go Fish!" he exclaimed, making each word its own sentence. "And I thought you were smart."

"He's joking," Grace said quickly, and then slapped Monroe on the leg. "Be nice," I heard her mutter before turning to me. Monroe and

I shared a glance, and I wondered what Grace would say if she knew of our recent interactions. I winced, thinking of the high-pitched earful I'd get if she found out those interactions had involved talking about her. "Just pay attention to what we're doing," Grace instructed. "You'll catch on fast."

It turned out that I had played Go Fish before, I just hadn't remembered its name. Go Fish was just as repetitive and seemingly pointless as Sorry had been, but I stayed quiet for Grace's sake.

"Got any ones?" I asked Monroe when it was my turn.

"Oh, I've got a one," Monroe responded with a lopsided grin. "In fact, I've met *the* one, and you're it." Grace slapped him on the leg again, and he yelped. "Sorry! I just couldn't help myself." Grace rolled her eyes and giggled. "No, I don't have any ones," he said eventually. "Go fish."

I drew a card as Grace began her turn. "So, Cassidy," she said after she had asked Monroe for fours. "I'm curious. Why do you work so hard in school?"

Although I was familiar with Grace's tendency to ask a serious question in a casual manner, I was still caught off guard. "What do you mean?"

"Are you doing it for yourself, or someone else?"

"A combination, I guess." Grace looked at me with wide eyes, and I realized I would be forced to elaborate. I cleared my throat, feeling the room become a little smaller. "It was definitely just for my parents at first. But now their goals have kind of transformed into my goals, so … I don't really remember ever feeling any other way."

Grace nodded and then gestured for Monroe to start his turn. "Why do you ask?" I blurted, cutting off Monroe as he was about to speak.

Grace's eyes shrank as she realized that the microscope had been turned on her. I could tell that she hated the attention as much as I did. "You have so much direction and focus," she said, her voice flat. "I had been wondering if that was something you had gotten all on your own."

"I don't know," I said. "But I don't think it'd be possible for me to lose it at this point, no matter how much I might want to."

"Why would you ever want to lose it?" Monroe said. The serious tone of his voice didn't match the nonchalant mold of his face, and I found it hard to accept that the two could coexist in one person. "You actually know what you want to do with your life. You're doing things for a purpose."

"Well, true. But aren't you?"

A smile grew on Monroe's face. "Yeah, but you want to know what my purpose is? Every little thing I do in life, I do to get girls to like me. I take challenging classes so that I will be able to talk with a girl about any subject that interests her. I take band because, let's face it, girls go crazy over musicians. I participate in P.E. so that I will become fit and therefore more physically attractive. I tell jokes so that girls will fall in love with my sense of humor." Here he stopped to place his hand on his chest, a bright smile on his face. "And it's all been in preparation for this moment, where I will now hit on you."

"Monroe," Grace scolded, slapping him again as I felt heat rise on my cheeks. "How many times do I have to tell you? Be nice."

"I thought that was incredibly nice! I just hit on her, she should be flattered."

Grace rolled her eyes and looked at me with a silent apology for her best friend's behavior. I felt my embarrassment shift into jealousy as I watched the two of them interact. For the first time, their closeness became noteworthy, and their companionship something I coveted.

"Wow," I said, swallowing the feeling. "I am both slightly disturbed and amazed by your dedication to your chosen purpose."

"Moving on," Monroe said, holding his palm up. "Now you've got to share, Grace. What's your purpose?"

Grace put down her cards, officially abandoning the moribund game, and began to wrap strands of hair around her index finger. "I want to be myself," she said after a moment. "In everything I do, I try to make sure I remain true to myself, no matter what."

I contemplated Grace's purpose. It was certainly not logical, but then again absolutely nothing was logical when it came to Grace. Her purpose was very specific and yet devoid of a clear plan of action. I wanted to mention all of these things to her, but when I opened my mouth, her eye caught mine, and I found myself saying, "That's interesting."

"Yeah, well," Grace muttered, "It's not really going to build a future."

"But it's working to preserve you as a person," Monroe said, patting Grace on the back.

"Is that better than having a future?" she asked. With her eyes so wide and her face so pale, I was able to clearly identify the emotion on her face for the first time. It was vulnerability. "Is that better?" Grace repeated, the question now clearly a dare for me to use my "never-ending knowledge." But I didn't know which was better, so I remained silent.

"Well, that reaches my limit of seriousness for the day," Monroe said after a lengthy silence. He brought his hands up and made a huge display of cracking his knuckles. "Now let's fish for some cards."

As Monroe grabbed our cards and began shuffling them together, Grace and I exchanged glances. I had never thought it would be possible to feel connected to her in any way, but in that moment I did.

"It's not an either-or situation, Grace," I said quietly. "Of *course* you'll have a future. *Everyone* has a future."

"I guess so," Grace said, biting her lip. "I guess."

chapter *15*

It took us half an hour to get ready for the party. Monroe put on black slacks and a button-down shirt and I wore the black and white dress that Grace had picked out. The real surprise was Grace herself, who emerged from her room in a pink ballet-style dress. It was cutesy, bright, and probably far too showy for the event we were going to. But obviously Grace didn't care, so I didn't mention it.

"I've never been to Stanford before," Monroe said as we all loaded into the Harpers' minivan. "I feel like by entering the campus I should automatically become smarter."

Grace flashed a smile. "If that were possible, then there would be way too many smart people in this world."

"You're joking, right?" I blurted after a useless minute of studying his face. "Please tell me that was a joke."

"Of course, Cassidy," Monroe said with a wink. "You can't take everything I say so seriously."

"Yeah, I don't think he's ever really been serious in his life," Grace said with a giggle, nudging Monroe with her elbow.

"Hey," he said, blocking her attack with his hand. "I'm just serious enough."

"All right, kids," Mr. Harper said, chiming in from the front of the car. "We're going to a serious event here. So let's tone down the joking and put our best feet forward."

"You got it, Dad," Cassidy said, straightening up and saluting him like a military cadet. I groaned, hoping that Likith had kept his promise to be there so that I wouldn't have to be around Grace and

never trust a happy song

Monroe all night. My feelings towards Grace had reverted from worry to exasperation, switching as fast as Grace's moods did.

The social night was being held in a large conference room filled with round tables and a little stage near the front. When we arrived, several families were already there, and people were mingling around the room.

"Oh joy, mingling," I muttered. "My favorite."

Grace giggled, even though nothing was funny. "Why do you hate it so much?"

I sighed before turning to her, a multitude of reasons swarming in my head. "One, mingling requires small talk, which is not really my forte. Second, that small talk usually leads to someone asking me about college, my major, or my GPA, all of which are things I would really rather not discuss."

Grace shrugged. "I don't really see anything too bad about that."

"You would if you had been coached over and over again on exactly what to say. It starts to feel like a mask." I swallowed then, realizing I needed to cut the conversation off now, or Grace would keep asking questions. "Let's look for Likith," I said, turning in a circle to scan the room.

Grace made an annoying 'ooo' sound. "Who's Likith?"

"He's my friend," I said slowly, giving her a sharp look. "While I'm looking for him, why don't you go track down Monroe? Make sure he doesn't knock the punch bowl over, or something."

"Okay," Grace said with a flip of her hair. She turned around and then immediately turned back to me, looking satisfied. "I already found him! He's over there, talking to that Indian guy."

"Oh, no," I said, looking in the direction she was indicating. Likith might find my annoyance with Grace amusing, but I suspected that he and Monroe would not be socially compatible. I walked over to them as fast as I could without running.

"It's simply not true!" Monroe was saying when I arrived, flourishing a hand in the air. "Traditional pick-up lines are so much better."

"No," Likith said in a tone I recognized as his 'I-think-you-are-dumb' voice. "They are cheesy and have absolutely no logical content. They're useless particles of filler."

"That's the point," Monroe said, clearly exasperated. "They're supposed to be cheesy!"

"Um, hi," I said.

"Cassidy!" Likith exclaimed, placing his hand on my shoulder. "Perfect. Help explain to this guy why scientific pick-up lines are so much better than normal ones."

"Uh, let's not argue about this here," I said, glancing about the room. "This is not the appropriate time or place."

"My thoughts exactly," Likith said, eyeing Monroe. "But this fellow over here decided to hit on a girl as she was serving herself punch."

"She literally asked me if I 'wanted some'!" Monroe exclaimed, his eyes twinkling. "I wasn't going turn down such a great set-up."

"It was a cheap set-up," Likith said. "Pick-up lines like that require no effort at all."

"Are we seriously arguing about this?" I snarled, stepping in between them. "You," I said, pointing at Monroe. "Go find Grace. And

never trust a *happy* song

you," I said, giving Likith a small smile. "I know it might be hard, but just let it go." Likith looked at me with annoyance as Monroe waved before walking away.

"He is so annoying. Such an idiot," Likith grumbled, stuffing his hands into his pockets.

"Ha!" I sang, poking his chest. "Now you know how I feel!"

"I highly doubt Grace is *that* annoying."

"Well, you can find out for yourself if you'd like," I said, scanning the room for Grace's pink dress.

When I turned back to Likith, he looked like I had told him that he had scored a five on all of his AP exams. "So she's here?"

"Yes. And that boy you just called an idiot is her best friend."

"Oh my God."

"Yes, they're quite a pair. Now come on," I said, grabbing his arm. "You kept saying you wanted to meet her, so let's get this over with."

Finding Grace wasn't difficult, as I turned to find both her and Monroe trotting straight towards us. "Can you please not run?" I asked in a harsh whisper once they reached Likith and me. "This is not a playground."

"Don't freak out," Grace managed to get out in between her breaths.

"Why would she freak out?" Monroe countered.

"I don't know. I just have a feeling she might."

"Wait," I said, holding up my hand before the two of them could get into an argument. "What is this thing I might or might not freak out about?"

[*119*]

Grace drew in a large breath and held it for a moment, her swollen cheeks making her look like a chipmunk. When she let it out, her words came at the same time. "Your mom's here."

My feet began to feel slightly numb. "What?"

"She's here. Meaning in this room, at this social-whatever thing."

"But," I began, my jaw moving up and down like a stalled machine. "How is that possible? Why did she come? How did she *get* here?" I looked around the room, expecting her to pop into view at any moment.

"I think Grace's parents invited her," Monroe said casually, unaware of the tension spreading through my muscles.

"She must have been worried after that phone conversation we had," I said to no one in particular, the unfortunate logic of it all mapping itself out in my head.

"What?" Grace asked, speaking over my rambling. "How would you know that?"

"God, I *knew* it was a mistake to call her! How could I have been so *stupid*?"

"Remember earlier today," Monroe began, his voice rising over mine, "when they said they'd planned a surprise for tonight?"

"And now she's going to come and see how everything is set up here …."

"Oh!" Grace exclaimed, dragging out the vowel. "That's right! I had just assumed my mom was planning on making some special cake for afterwards or something."

"Well, apparently not," I snapped, not feeling the humor. "Apparently she decided to invite my mother." I stepped back from them, feeling almost dizzy. "God, my mother is going to freak when she sees all of this."

"All of what?" Monroe asked.

"You!" I exclaimed, feeling panic bubble up with my words. "You, and Grace, and Grace's family. Don't get me wrong, you guys are great people. You are kind and generous and hard-working, but you are not what my mom wants for me."

"What, so we're not good enough for you?" Grace asked, her voice sounding so hurt that I was afraid to look at her. I didn't want to be a person who put that look on her face.

"No, no …." I fumbled as always, not knowing how to translate my fears into words.

"Cassidy," I heard Likith say, reminding me that he too was here for this soap opera. What should have been a perfectly stress-free night was quickly turning into an absolute nightmare.

"Oh right, I forgot," I said with as much enthusiasm as I could muster. "Likith, Grace. Grace, Likith."

"Hi!" Grace chirped, bouncing on her toes.

Likith cracked a smile, and I knew what was coming. "I must say, I know my chemistry, and you've got one significant figure."

"Really, man?" Monroe asked. "You're going to do that just to spite me?"

Likith straightened, the top of his head now almost stretching over mine. "I've been a proud distributor of knowledge-based pick-up lines for years. If you think that the only reason I said that was to spite you, then you've seriously miscalculated."

"Everyone, stop!" I said. "I see my mother." Everyone turned in the direction I was facing as I stared at her approaching figure. She waved at me without smiling, which made the gesture look much less friendly.

Okay, look composed, I commanded. *She expects you to be composed and smart and hard working. Not flustered and emotionally involved and dealing with all of this crap. Think about velocity. Simple, straight-forward velocity: a function of distance and time. If I travel the 35 feet to her in 15 seconds, I'll be traveling at a velocity of roughly 2.33 feet per second.*

"Okay, maybe you should calm down a bit before you talk to her," Grace said, interrupting my attempt to transform into a more composed Cassidy. But it was too late, because I – the new, flustered, emotional Cassidy that I had metamorphosed into – was already dashing past Monroe and Grace to meet Mom halfway.

chapter *16*

When I reached my mother, my already minimal conversational skills disappeared entirely. With nothing of substance to say, I settled on a weak, "Hi, Mom."

"Surprise!" she said, placing her hand on my shoulder.

"Well, I am surprised," I said, making my voice sound as normal as possible.

"You sound stressed," Mom said. She paused to formulate her thoughts. "I can't decide if that's a good or a bad thing."

"I thought you weren't visiting until July," I said, though I knew better.

"I was concerned after our last phone call. Something in your voice just didn't sound right. And then the Harpers invited me to come out for this social night. Apparently you're going to receive an award?"

"It's not a sure thing," I muttered. I had never hated the Harpers' overzealous optimism more than in that moment.

"It should be," Mom said, giving me a small smile. "You should be the best." The statement fell somewhere in between an endearment and a threat. The line was rather fuzzy with her.

"There will always be people who are better than me," I said. "You know that. People who started earlier or are just naturally smarter."

"You can't think that way, Cassidy," Mom said, pinning me with her gaze like I was a bacterium on a microscope slide. "I was hoping this summer would eliminate that attitude. You need to be confident in your skills. That's what makes the difference between a student who's smart and a student who's outstanding. It can make the difference between a 3.9 GPA and a 4.0, an A on an exam versus an A-plus."

"I know that," I muttered weakly. Then, "Mom, did you come here just to lecture me?" I had fallen into the trap of missing my mother, until the moment she returned and I realized how much she relished the role of educational coach. For the first time I felt the full burn of my hatred for that trap.

Mom let out a sigh, no doubt thinking how annoyingly adolescent I sounded. I was thinking the same thing, while simultaneously wondering how my emotions had gotten so out of control.

"I was also worried about you," she said, putting her arm around me. She gave me an awkward one-sided hug before releasing me from her hold. "I know it can be difficult to work so hard during the summer, especially when you have the most difficult year of high school coming up."

I hadn't even been thinking about that, but her comment sent my blood pressure soaring. "Not what I need to be thinking about now, Mom," I muttered, directing my gaze to the floor.

"Think of it this way," Mom said, once again placing her hand on my shoulder. Its weight felt like the source of all the tension rushing through me, the area under her fingertips pulsating with stress. "This summer is supposed to help you prepare for next year. It will give you another leg up in the competition. You'll have more experience with what these colleges are looking for."

"Trust me, I keep telling myself that. It's just that," and here I looked down again, as though the floor was a better place to direct this

never trust a *happy* song

sentiment, "sometimes, being all the way out here, I find myself wondering why I'm doing what I'm doing. I thought I knew what the purpose of all this was, but now it's all distorted in my head. When I'm at school it's obvious to me why I work so hard, because everyone else is doing it too, but here ...."

I trailed off, only able to focus on the pressure of Mom's grip, which had tightened with every word. Her fingers began to flutter slightly, a Morse code that allowed me to feel her next words coming.

"I'm requesting that you switch to another host family."

"No!" I said in unison with her last words. "No."

"Yes," she stressed. "I was wrong. They aren't a good match for you."

For a split second, I was overwhelmed with happiness at the fact that Mom had admitted she was wrong about something. But then the circumstances came rushing back, and this victory was overshadowed by the loss that came with it.

"Meaning they aren't all obsessed with schooling," I said, wishing she would just come right out and say it.

"Meaning they aren't good for you."

"Mom, you just don't like the fact that they think there's more to life than school!"

"Plus, I'm not sure their daughter does very well in school," she half-whispered, motioning to Grace with her eyes. I looked over at Grace as she and Monroe fought over the punch ladle. I got that odd pang in my heart again as I watched them shove each other with wide smiles on their faces. And then I was overcome with anger.

"What does that have to do with it?" I said harshly. "She's still a perfectly fine person."

"She's not the kind of person who gets into the Ivy Leagues," Mom said, her voice still frustratingly calm.

"So suddenly she's a failure because she doesn't have a 4.0 GPA?" I practically yelled. My voice was now so loud that it caught Grace's attention, who turned to find Mom and me staring at her. I quickly turned my gaze away. "Getting B's or C's in school doesn't make her a dumb person."

"I never said it did," Mom said, still calm. "I just was using it as an example of how the Harpers' lifestyle is so different from the kind you need to lead."

It was true, but that didn't mean I wanted to agree with her. "Don't make me change host families," I pleaded. "Please, let me stay with the Harpers." I wasn't exactly sure why I wanted to stay, but I knew that I couldn't let her make me switch. Maybe, deep down, I had loved the Harpers all along. Maybe I didn't want to leave Grace now. Or maybe I didn't want Mom to take another thing away from me to make me focus more on school.

Mom gave me a look, like her pupils could cut through my forehead to see what I was thinking. That was her one shortcoming; she could always tell how stressed out I was and how much work I had left to do, but she never could figure out what I was thinking. "Are you sure this is what you want?" she asked, and I couldn't believe that I might win.

"Yes."

never trust a *happy* song

"Because I'd gotten the feeling that you and Grace don't exactly get along."

"We do get along." It was such a lie, but one worth telling if it would allow me to stay.

"And I don't want to get any more phone calls about how you're questioning your direction."

"You won't."

"And you're going to retake the SAT IIs?"

"I–"

"You're going to retake the SAT IIs?" Mom said again, stressing each individual word so that they became bullets.

I so desperately did not want to retake the SAT IIs. I did not want to have to re-prove that I could be perfect, nor did I buy into the idea that accomplishing something as a junior means more than accomplishing it as a sophomore. But at that moment, I wanted nothing more than to stay with the Harpers. So before I could properly analyze the sacrifice, I found myself saying, "I will."

"Fine," Mom said, "then you can stay with them."

"Thank you," I said calmly, knowing that Mom would prefer me to stay cool and collected, even though I wanted to jump up and down as though I'd just aced a big exam. I reveled in my disguised happiness until the crackling of a microphone pulled me back into reality.

"Attention," a woman said. "If everyone could take their seats, we will begin."

"You go ahead and sit down," Mom said. "I've got to go to the bathroom."

"Okay. It's right down the hall to the left."

"Thank you, Cass," she said, swooping her head down to kiss me on the cheek. Her shortening of my name felt unnatural and I winced. After she walked away I let out a large breath. Arguing with Mom was a supreme test – harder than any final exam or timed essay. After an argument with her, I usually felt more frustrated than when we'd started. Though technically I had won this time, it was frustrating that we even had to argue about such a thing.

Monroe and Grace had already sat down at a table, though Grace's parents were nowhere to be seen. "Are you okay?" Grace asked when I sat down next to her with a sigh.

"Yes," I said. "I'm fine."

"Seriously," Grace repeated. "Are you okay?"

I clenched my jaw, not in the mood. "If you just asked the question and I gave you an answer, then why are you repeating it?"

"Uh," Grace began, "is this a trick question?"

I sighed. "Look, can you just not talk for a couple of minutes? I know that's probably really hard for you, but I'd appreciate it." It was ridiculous, I knew, not to want to interact with a girl that I'd just sacrificed so much to spend more time with. But the crowd in the room was beginning to overwhelm me, the buzz of their chatter increasing to a roar in my ears.

"So you *do* have relationship issues with your mom," Grace said after a moment, whispering over the woman's voice that was once again echoing through the speakers.

"No, I don't," I said.

"I saw the way you two were arguing."

"I thought I asked you to be quiet," I hissed, glaring at her. She stared back at me with perfectly clear eyes, not scared off by my mood. "We normally get along fine." But as I said the words, I realized it was not true. We clashed over a multitude of issues – what was a good enough grade on a test, what my class rank needed to be, whether I had spent enough time studying – but normally I chose not to fight back. "We ... we just ..." I folded my sweaty hands over each other, not sure what to say. "All right, fine. We argue. Our relationship isn't perfect. Is that what you wanted to hear?"

Grace shrugged. "I'm just saying that maybe you're more like a normal teenager than you think."

I sighed and looked at Grace again. We stared at each other for a while, my face surely not as pleasant as hers. "What is *normal*?" I asked eventually, though I didn't really want an answer.

"For the record," Grace whispered, leaning over so that her elbows were braced against the table, "you did freak out."

I gave her a look that I hoped made it clear I was not in the mood. A multitude of worries coursed through my body and settled in the pit of my stomach. "I'm feeling kind of sick," I said, making a face.

Grace inched forward in her seat. "Do you think you're going to throw up?"

"I don't know, but my mouth feels gross. I feel like I need to brush my teeth."

"You can if you want," Grace said, grabbing her little purse and shaking it in front of my face like it was a bell. "I've got a toothbrush."

I pushed her bag down, not wanting to attract attention. "You brought a toothbrush to the social night?"

"I bring a toothbrush everywhere," Grace said with a shrug.

"O-kay," I drawled. "That's odd." She gave me a weak smile before looking down to dig through her bag.

"No, no," I said, reaching out to shut the bag again. "There's no need. I'll be fine. Beta-hemolytic streptococcus, remember?"

Grace giggled. "Beta-hemolytic streptococcus."

I was about to comment on how she had butchered the pronunciation, when my mother arrived at the table. When I looked up, I saw Mr. and Mrs. Harper standing behind her. I swallowed, feeling nervous at the thought of them having a conversation about me. If Mrs. Harper told Mom about my snapping at Grace or my semi-breakdown, Mom would probably back out on her promise to let me stay.

"You have two weeks," Mom whispered after she sat down next to me.

"Two weeks for what?"

Mom unfolded her napkin and placed it on her lap, though there was no sign of food arriving. "Two weeks to prove to me that staying with the Harpers isn't a distraction. In two weeks I'll visit again to check on you."

"Okay," I said. I hoped that I could actually get it together in two weeks, and started making a checklist of everything I needed to do. *Less play, more studying. And definitely finish the big research paper by then.*

"Okay," Mom repeated, signaling that the conversation was over. I breathed out again, telling myself to worry about Mom later, and tried to pay attention to what the lady on the stage was saying.

chapter *17*

"Well, that was fascinating," Likith said to me dryly as we walked down the hallway outside the banquet room. The woman had talked for twenty minutes about the summer program, what the students were getting out of it, and how it would help them succeed not just in school but in life. At the end of her speech, she briefly mentioned two students who had gotten 104 percent in the course so far. Then large portions of food were whisked onto the tables and the small talk resumed. That was it. No awards. No significance.

"My mom's upset," I told Likith, staring at my feet as we walked. I tried to align each one perfectly in front of the other, as if I was on a balance beam.

"Oh?"

"I think she expected me to get some kind of award. I think that's a big part of the reason she came. She'd never admit it, though," I said with a shrug. "But I suspect it nonetheless."

"That's a pretty depressing thought," Likith said, "her coming more for an award than for you."

"You're surprised?" I couldn't help asking, raising my eyebrows.

Likith cracked a grin. "No, I've been there. But it is depressing, nonetheless."

I shrugged. "It seems pretty normal to me. Once I fell down the stairs at school, and she came to make sure that I wasn't too badly hurt to take the PSAT that afternoon. I'm not trying to say she doesn't love me, it's just …." I trailed off, looking up from my feet to Likith's face. "It's kind of scary sometimes how obsessed she is with this stuff."

"Aren't we the same?" Likith asked. He gestured between us, but his eyes stared straight ahead. Even from the side, he looked sad, almost forlorn. "Isn't that all we think about, too?"

"I suppose," I said. "I guess it doesn't seem so strange that *we* think about it. What else are we going to think about?"

Likith let out a laugh and nudged me in the side. "Our friends? Our booming social life?"

"Pfft," I said, sending air out through my teeth. I gave him a big grin. "What friends?"

At that moment we reached the end of the hall. "I guess we should go back," I said reluctantly. It was nice to be out in the hallway with Likith, where I could pretend it was a world without futures or obligations. Likith nodded, and we were about to turn around when Grace came out of the nearby restroom.

"Oh my stars," she said as she almost bumped into us. "What are you guys doing down here?"

"We found the atmosphere in there stifling," Likith said with a tiny smile.

"Are you all right?" I asked. Grace looked rather run down, her skin rough where it was normally smooth and her usual vivaciousness absent. As I noticed those abnormalities, I realized that I never used to notice such details. I wondered if this was what Mom meant by distractions: those little things about people that don't really matter, but sometimes do.

"Yep," she said twirling a piece of her hair. "I am A-okay."

"You're what?" I asked, not sure if I had misheard her or not.

never trust a *happy* song

"Okay, Cassidy," she said, her smile returning. "I'm okay." I was about to respond when her face went blank, her eyes widening to a scary size. "Oh my stars," she whispered. "They're everywhere."

I turned to follow the path of her wide eyes. A tall, skinny girl was walking down the hallway towards us. A few seconds of deduction connected Grace's alarmed face with the girl's elongated figure, and I realized she must be another of *them*.

"Grace the Disgrace!" Mean Girl exclaimed, opening her arms as if going in for a hug. "Fancy meeting you here."

"Hi," Grace said, studying her feet. I watched as she placed one foot slightly over the other, and wondered if she missed her rain boots.

"Let me guess, your family is doing one of these stupid host family things as well?" Mean Girl embellished the phrase "host family" with air quotes, as if it wasn't a real thing. I felt myself getting mad.

"Yes," Grace answered, still examining her footwear.

"Well, it's nice to see you out of your overalls," Mean Girl said. "Now it's obvious that you have a figure. I could never tell with those baggy things. You could've been fat underneath them or something."

I tried to imagine getting up in the morning and worrying about what I was wearing, or whether I looked like I had a figure. Whether I had one or not, it wasn't going to affect the success of my day. That depended on other things, like sufficient sleep and completing my work. I wondered if this girl ever thought about those things.

Grace took a deep breath, puffing her cheeks out before letting the air go. "Well, that's all fine and dandy," she said shakily, "but I don't care what you think about me."

"Funny," the girl shot back, "because it sure sounds like you do."

Grace's large eyes became shiny, and for a horrible moment I thought she was going to cry. I had no idea why this confrontation was happening or how it was going to end, and I turned away in an effort to clear my head. The image of Grace saying that she just wanted to be herself replayed in my head. My fists clenched as a thought rocketed into my mind: these girls were trying to ruin that. When my eyes refocused, I saw Monroe standing at the end of the hallway, staring at the scene behind me. I motioned for Monroe to come over and somehow make the girl go away. Monroe nodded, but instead of walking over, he began to run.

For a moment I froze, staring as Monroe hurtled towards us. Then I jolted awake and leaped out of the way, towing an obviously uncomfortable Likith. Grace must have seen Monroe coming, because she shouted, "Monroe!"

Mean Girl turned around at the split second that Monroe collided with her. First their torsos slammed together, and then they smacked heads hard enough to send them both crashing to the floor.

"Ow!" Monroe yelped, grabbing his head.

"Oh my God," Mean Girl exclaimed, standing up and helping Monroe to his feet. "I am so sorry."

Monroe paused for a second, staring at her, before cracking a wide smile. "Oh no, it's not your fault. I was knocked off my feet by the sight of you."

"Oh my God," I whispered, rolling my eyes. Likith snickered as Monroe smiled even wider, looking very proud of himself. Mean Girl, on the other hand, was clearly not amused, and let out a sound of disgust. She pushed Monroe out of the way with one hand while flipping her ponytail over her shoulder with the other, so that her hair whipped Monroe in the face.

"Nice to meet you!" Monroe called after her, his smile unwavering. However, as soon as she turned the corner, his smile faded. "She's stupid, Grace," he said, taking the words right out of my mouth. "You shouldn't listen to her."

"I know," Grace said. I felt that it would be good to also say "*Don't* listen to her," but I couldn't make the words come.

"She sounds like a delight," Likith said, clearing his throat. "Does she go to your school?"

"Yeah," Grace said.

Likith nodded. "I'm sorry."

"Yeah."

Then there was silence, and I picked at the skirt of my dress, wondering how to move on. "You've got to admit," Monroe said after a moment, "that was pretty damn smooth."

Grace giggled, a good sign. "Smoother than you pointing it out just now."

"I'm sorry, I'm just so proud. I'm so excited and I just can't hide it." Monroe did a little dance with his arms, jumping from one foot to the other.

Likith rolled his eyes. "Yeah, almost as smooth as that fall after you collided with her."

"I'm going to ignore your sarcasm and admit that, yes, it did hurt a little bit. I think I'm still suffering from deceleration trauma."

Likith cleared his throat again. "Deceleration trauma happens when a very long fall is followed by sudden deceleration. Therefore it does not apply to your situation because, one, your fall was not very long and, two, you did not suffer major deceleration."

"I beg to differ."

"Then you beg to be wrong."

Monroe just blinked in response, and I laughed out loud, the sound feeling good as it left my lips. "Wow," Grace said after a moment. "He's like your twin."

Likith rolled his eyes and leaned over to me. "Wow. His idiocy *truly* defies gravity."

I was about to once again ask Grace if she was okay, when my mom's voice echoed down the hallway.

"Cassidy," she said, "you need to come back and be social. It's rude to loiter out here."

"Okay," I called over my shoulder. "That's my cue," I said, forcing a smile. "I'll see you guys later."

"I need to go as well," Likith said. I gave him a look, suspecting he didn't want to be stuck with Monroe.

"You and Likith should come over sometime and hang out with me and Monroe," Grace said, her eyes regaining some sparkle. "We could play games."

Likith popped an eyebrow. "*Games*?"

"Or even study, if that's what you really want," Grace said, rolling her eyes. Then I heard her mutter, "My stars."

"Uh, sure," Likith said, giving me a look. I felt trapped between Grace's hopeful eyes and Mom's laser pointer gaze on my back.

"I've really got to go," I managed, backing away.

never trust a happy song

Grace must have said, "Okay," because her voice echoed in my ears as I turned and walked straight towards my mom.

"Who were those people?" Mom whispered once I reached her at the door.

"Just some friends." I said the word without thinking it through, and immediately saw my mistake in Mom's responding gaze.

"You have time for friends outside of school?"

"No, I mean," I stuttered, "it was Grace and her friend Monroe, plus a boy I know from the program."

"Oh," she said with a nod. She gestured for me to go back into the auditorium, and as I walked in I thought about how much better it felt to call them friends.

chapter *18*

Mom left as abruptly as she had arrived. She came back to the Harpers' house with us after the social, but then quickly announced that she needed to be on her way.

"I need to be at the office tomorrow, so I'm driving back tonight," she said when Mrs. Harper inquired about where she was staying the night.

"Oh, but that's such a long drive!" Mrs. Harper said. "Why don't you just spend the night here and leave early in the morning? We have an extra guest bedroom and we'd be delighted to have you."

"No, no," Mom said, backing up as Mrs. Harper advanced on her. "That's a very nice offer, but I'm fine. And since my first meeting is at 8 o'clock, I'd have to leave before dawn."

"Well," Mrs. Harper said, chewing on her lip. "All right. We understand."

"See you in two weeks, Mom," I said, hugging her. I felt her lightly press her hands to my back.

"See you in two weeks," she repeated.

Each day the following week, I came home to find Monroe already at the Harper household, playing a game with Grace in my room. Forced to find new places to study, I discovered that no matter which room I chose, they followed me.

"Could you guys not do that here?" I asked in exasperation as I sat at the dining table. I was trying to choose my research paper topic,

never trust a happy song

but my progress was hindered by Monroe and Grace playing a very passionate game of Battleship.

"Just a moment," Monroe said, holding up his finder. "I say A4."

"No!" Grace howled, burying her head in her hands. "You sunk my battleship."

"Yes!" Monroe yelled, stretching out the word long enough for him to jump up and down on his chair three times. "Take that, sucker!"

"I'm trying to work here," I huffed, although I couldn't hide the beginning of a smile.

"Well, that's your first problem," Grace said with a giggle. I swatted her foot with mine under the table, but that only made her giggle more.

"Grace," I whined.

"Okay, okay. How about this, before Monroe and I start another round, we will try to help you."

"No," I said immediately. "That is not a good idea."

"What?" Monroe said, clasping his hand to his chest. "You don't think we're smart enough?"

"No," I groaned, hating that guilt trip. "That's not what I meant!"

"Chill, Cassidy," Monroe said. "I was only joshing." He jumped down from his chair and resettled on it cross-legged. "Now, what assignment is causing you to waste this lovely summer day?"

Monroe looked at me expectantly, and I stared back. After a minute I deduced that even their help would be better than their continuing to make a racket. "Okay," I said, adjusting myself into a similar position. "I have this huge research paper due at the end of the month, and I'm trying to decide what to write about."

"Pause," Monroe said, holding up his hand. "Is this an all-encompassing research paper, or does it have to be narrowed to a certain topic?"

"I have to write about how the properties of physics affect some object's activity, or allow it to work."

"Ew," Grace said, wrinkling her nose. "That sounds boring."

Monroe nodded at her. "Definitely not a joyful way to spend one's time. But we promised we'd help her."

Grace placed a finger on her chin and her gaze flitted up towards the ceiling. "How about how a boomerang works?" she suggested after a moment.

"I think that might be too simple," I replied. "It has to be fifteen to twenty pages."

"Oh my stars," Grace exclaimed, and she dropped her head onto the table.

"Okay. How about the physics of thunderstorms?" Monroe suggested.

I frowned. "I don't know. That topic doesn't really resonate with me, and I want to make sure I actually learn something interesting."

"Okay," Monroe said without skipping a beat. "How a hair dryer works?"

"No, that would be too dull."

"The human heart?"

"I've already studied that too many times."

"Darts?"

"Definitely not."

"How about how refrigerator magnets work?" Grace said, overlapping Monroe's next suggestion. "Like my word magnets, or the other bendable ones we use to hold up grocery lists."

I stopped short, my negative response dying on my lips. The idea seemed simplistic, and yet so unequivocally Grace-like that there was a chance of it being interesting.

"Elaborate," I requested.

"Well, I don't know," Grace said with a shrug. "I mean, I've never taken physics, but there must be some kind of property responsible for how they work, right? What keeps them anchored to the fridge?"

"I think that's just magnetism," I said, scratching my head.

"Okay, but why don't they slide downwards? Like, the magnet might keep it attached to the refrigerator surface, but that doesn't explain why it sticks to the same spot, even if there's a piece of paper behind it. And aren't magnets supposed to be metal, so why do ours bend?"

I frowned, trying to replay in my head all the physics laws that I had ever learned. "I'm not sure," I admitted.

"Wow," Grace said. She let out a breathy giggle. "I can't believe you just said that."

"So, refrigerator magnets?" Monroe asked, opening up his battleship board. "Because if you guys are all decided, I want to play another game and beat Grace again."

I deliberated for a moment, estimating the chance of coming up with a better idea. "I guess I'm writing about refrigerator magnets."

"Don't sound so sad about it!" Grace said. "Refrigerator magnets can be very fascinating."

"I hope so," I said, "because I'm going to be spending a lot of time writing about them."

"So are we done here?" Monroe asked, his question punctuated by antsy taps of his foot on the floor.

"Wait, one more thing!" Grace exclaimed, edging forward in her chair. "I almost forgot to tell you. I've been invited to a Fourth of July party. It sounds really fun, so I think we should go." At the word 'party', I knew it was time to exit the conversation and return to my work. I looked back down at my worksheet and set my sights on a new problem.

"Who's *we*?" I heard Monroe ask. *Maglev trains are an application of electromagnetism that combines magnets, electricity, and gravity.*

Grace shrugged. "I don't know. All of us, I guess. The invitation just said to bring whoever."

A Maglev train is 'levitated' by magnetic fields that oppose each other with a force equal to that of gravity. How much current would have to be sent through the circuit in order to create a magnetic force strong enough to support the weight of a 100-ton train car?

"Aha," Monroe said. "And who sent this mysterious invitation?"

As much as I tried to concentrate, my attention was flickering between physics and Grace, who shrugged again. She latched onto a strand of her hair and spun it around her finger. "Someone from school," she said. "Did you not get the same e-mail?" Monroe shook his head. "Huh. That's odd."

never trust a happy song

"So when is this party?" he asked. "I assume it's not being held on the actual Fourth of July."

I struggled to divert my attention away from them. *Back to physics, Cassidy. Physics makes trains move forward. Parties don't.*

"No, it's the day after."

"Oh," Monroe said, and then quickly looked down.

Grace narrowed her eyes. "What?"

Monroe continued to stare at the floor, and began to fiddle with the drawstring of his sweatpants. "Sorry, Grace, but I can't go."

"What?" she whined, dragging out the vowel. Then she froze, her mouth still open. "Wait, don't tell me ...."

Monroe nodded, confirming whatever she was thinking. I suspected I knew what he would say next and, wanting to avoid that conversation, I forced my eyes back to the worksheet. When Monroe spoke again, his voice was very quiet. "My dad scheduled tutoring for that night."

"And he won't let you change it?" Grace asked with a pout.

"Definitely not. You know my dad's big on his schedules."

"Ugh!" Grace slumped back in her chair and crossed her arms. "I can't believe you are deserting me for something school-related," she muttered.

Silence fell. After the quiet dragged on for an unusually long time, an uncomfortable sensation started to build in my forehead. I began to breathe very quietly, not wanting to look up, but certain that Grace's eyes had settled on me. My thought process sped up, as if mimicking the speed at which I wished my feet were taking me away. "So that means *you* are going to come," Grace said eventually, poking me in the arm. I jolted up and saw that she had leaned so far across the table so that she was practically lying on it.

"Oh, no," I said, scooting my chair away from the table. "I most certainly am not."

"And *why* not?" she demanded. I began to reply, but Grace's hand shot out and wrapped around my wrist. "Think about your answer carefully, because if you say 'I have to study' or 'I need to do my work,' I swear ...."

Her voice trailed off in a way that suggested a threat to my person, but I couldn't imagine Grace ever following through with a damaging act. I tried to muffle my resulting smile. "I have to do the research for this paper, Grace," I said as gently as possible. "You know that."

"Ugh," she groaned, laying her head down on the table. "You suck. I can't believe you're letting your mom scare you into spending all your time on schoolwork. You'd been making progress!"

"What?" I sputtered. "That is not what happened! I would have insisted on working on my paper no matter what!"

"Oh really?" Grace said, her eyebrows raised. "I saw how you two were arguing at the party. She definitely was unhappy about something."

"That's ridiculous," I said, leaning forward to match Grace's competitive stance. We stared each other down for a minute, but eventually her unwavering gaze broke through my confidence. "Okay, that's true," I conceded softly, wondering what Grace would do if she knew what was making my mother unhappy. "But that doesn't mean that she's forcing me to study. These are all my own decisions."

never trust a happy song

"Ugh," Grace groaned again. "I can't believe she's fooled you into thinking that." Grace pushed herself back across the table top until she fell onto her chair. "Monroe, help me out here."

My eyes flitted to Monroe, who sat with his legs bent up in front of him, his back slouched low in his chair. I recognized the look on his face as one I had worn many times, a clear warning that he did not want to get involved in this conversation.

"Look," Monroe began. "I don't really want to get in the middle of this. I understand what Grace is saying because, like, my parents get mad at me sometimes if they think I'm not working hard enough, and then I'll start studying a ton and it makes me think, 'Am I doing this for them or for me?' And sometimes I feel like I don't even know, like it's hard to tell the difference." He shrugged and simultaneously reached up to adjust his glasses as they slipped down. "All I know for sure is that it's weird when adults, like, care about stuff. It freaks me out that they can be so passionate about our future. What happened to parents not wanting their kids to grow up?"

Monroe had been avoiding eye contact during his speech, but then he looked right at me. I gaped at him, shocked that something so insightful had come from a boy who primarily prided himself on his pursuit of girls.

"All right, I'm finished," he said, holding up his hands. "That reaches my seriousness limit for the month."

Grace nodded and then looked at me, her eyes narrowed. "So will you come to the party? At least for a little bit?"

"No."

"Cassidy!" Grace closed her eyes and sighed. "Didn't you hear what Monroe said?"

Grace now sounded genuinely upset, and I faltered for a moment. "Yes, I did," I exclaimed once I had regained my focus. "And it was very insightful. But that doesn't change the fact that *I need to work on my paper.*"

"And what, the world would end if you didn't work on it for one night?"

"Not the world, but lots of bad things could happen."

Grace gripped the edge of the table as she leaned towards me. "Like what?"

The question was obviously a challenge. I sat up straighter, carefully thought it through, and gave the complete answer in a single deep breath. "Who knows what homework I'm going to get next week. I could get so much that I'm unable to spend any time on the paper. If so, I wouldn't be able to start writing it until the last minute, in which case it would be very low quality. And if I get a bad grade on the paper, my grade for the entire program will drop, because this paper is like our final exam. And I don't even want to *think* about what a bad grade on my transcript could do. The colleges I apply to could very well decide that I'm not good enough for their schools because of that one bad grade. So going to the party could compromise my entire future."

This line of reasoning was engraved in my mind, so that if there ever was a moment when I didn't feel like working, I could remind myself of the importance of not being lazy. I could not afford to be lazy, not when one slip-up could determine so much.

never trust a *happy* song

Grace gaped at me, and I braced myself for her horrified response. But instead she just shook her head and said, very quietly, "Does she make you think that way?"

"What do you mean?"

"Does your mother tell you that, whenever she thinks you're not working hard enough? Don't you see? She's brainwashing you!"

"Grace," I scolded. "That's ridiculous. She's just helping me look out for my future."

"Yes, and is it your future, or hers?"

"That's not a valid point," I said softly, stuck between defending Mom and defending myself. "Of course it's mine."

"So this is the kind of future you want? One where you look back and see that you spent your entire time in high school working for one thing? Is it your future or hers?"

"Okay, Grace, I get your point," I barked. "And if you must know, I've never thought about it that way. But you're being unfair! It's not like you're never influenced by your parents and your school!"

"Yes, but they're not trying to push something on me that will take over my entire life."

I shook my head, unable to reply. "Just forget it," Grace said, scooting her chair back. "Come on, Monroe. I'll play you in Battlefield."

I looked at Monroe, and felt very sorry for him. He looked incredibly uncomfortable, though I had heard him say multiple times that the Harpers' house was his second home. But here I was, making it uncomfortable for everyone. This, I understood, was why it was better to study alone.

natalie bina

As I sat frozen, Monroe glanced nervously at Grace before rising. He avoided my gaze by looking down and fiddling with his glasses. Grace gave me one last glare before stalking off, leaving me to sit alone with my new doubts in a house that wasn't mine.

chapter *19*

Grace gave me the silent treatment, and I hated it. It was eerie not to be greeted by her voice every time I entered a room. A few times, I wanted to approach her and break the silence, but when I was home she was either at diving practice or taking a shower. So it became a repeat of our previous fight, where afterward we stopped pushing each other and instead danced around the issues.

Worse than the silence was the relentless debate that Grace had started in my head. They kept me awake, these questions of 'What am I doing?' and 'What am I working for?' and, worst of all, 'Who am I doing it for?' These questions burrowed into my skull, making themselves at home so quickly that I wondered if they had been there all along. *And if they were,* I thought, *why didn't I notice them before?*

I spent more and more time at Stanford. After class I would go to the library, and stay until a staff member told me to leave. This meant that the only social activity I had to endure during the day was dinner. After that was over, I could flee to my room and work in solitude.

I knew Mom would be happy with this development. Less distraction means more time to work, she would say. But knowing it would please her only made me sadder. As I tried to concentrate on the physical properties of refrigerator magnets, I found myself questioning why a lack of friends and general human interaction would please a mother. It was, again, interesting, but (a) not related to physics and (b) not helping me write my introductory paragraph.

Concentrate, Cassidy, I pleaded with myself. *You must concentrate.*

"I thought of a great one yesterday," Likith said as I desperately tried to focus on a math problem.

"A great what?" I asked. *The inverse tangent of the angle should give me its value. So if I can just find two sine and cosine values that multiply to 1...*

"Pick-up line," Likith said, giving me a look. "Haven't you been listening?"

I didn't answer, not wanting to admit how spaced out I'd been the last couple of days. I squinted, trying to focus on the small print of the worksheet. The motion made a nerve ending at the top of my head begin beating like a drum. Stress plus a lack of sleep was making my eyes feel like they were bleeding out of my head. *FOCUS!* I commanded. *The angle has to be in the second quadrant of the unit circle.*

"Anyways," Likith said after a while, making me aware that he had probably been watching my struggle. "Here it is." He cleared his throat and I cringed, knowing he was going to say the line in his "smooth" voice, which he claimed was sexy. "You have nicer legs than an isosceles right triangle."

I gave him a look to show him I was not amused, and then looked back down to my paper. *And $\frac{\sqrt{2}}{2}$ times $\frac{2}{\sqrt{2}}$ cancels out to be 1. So the angle must be 45°!*

"Don't you get it?" he asked.

"Yes, Likith. I get it." I moved on to the next problem, and tried to comprehend the figures on the page.

never trust a *happy* song

"Come on, Cassidy," he said, drawing out his words. "You've got to admit it's pretty funny."

"What are we doing?" I asked in exasperation, pushing down so hard on the page of unintelligible equations that the tip of my pencil broke.

"Um, doing our math homework?" Likith asked, pointing to our worksheets with his un-broken pencil.

"No, I mean with our lives."

Likith blinked several times before beginning to drum his fingers against the table. "Well, uh …" He scratched his head, and I thought that this was the first time I had ever seen him at a loss for an eloquent response. "That's a very big question, Cassidy."

"I've been thinking about it recently," I said. "Why are we working our butts off now so that we can go to one specific college and study one specific thing, without even getting the chance to experiment and explore life and find out what we actually like?" I pretended to find my fingers very interesting as I spoke. I didn't want to see the look on Likith's face, in case he thought I sounded stupid. He was silent for a very long time, and I feared that it had been a ridiculous question for me to ask, especially to him. After all, we were both in summer school at one of the world's top universities, which implicitly meant we were okay with devoting our free time to yet more work.

"I don't know," he said eventually. "I mean, I was raised knowing that that was how I was going to spend my time in high school, if not the majority of my life. In my family, success is measured by academic accomplishments."

"That's how my mom feels now," I said. "But when I was younger, she never talked about it." I paused, straining to remember my elementary and middle school years. "I used to have friends over on the weekends," I said, and burst into giggles. Likith began to laugh with me, although it didn't really seem like laughter.

"I never really did," he said once the moment had subsided, "unless we were getting tutored together."

"That's so sad."

"I know." Likith smiled, and it was perhaps the saddest smile that I had ever seen. "So are you saying that you miss having a life that's not focused on grades and standardized test scores?"

"I didn't before," I said after a while. "But I think I'm starting to."

"It's from living with that family, isn't it?" Likith asked. I had been prepared to say no, but as his words clicked into place in my head, I realized they were true.

"They laugh so much," I said. "Monroe and Grace. They're always talking and laughing, and doing the most random pointless things." I had to smile, thinking about how they had argued over their game of Battleship, as if it was real ships that they had torpedoed. "It feels really good to laugh," I said, more to myself than to Likith. "I'd forgotten how good it feels."

"Yeah?"

"Yeah. It makes me think I should laugh more."

Likith grinned. "If only it were socially acceptable to start laughing at our math homework."

That reminded me of the work I was supposed to be doing instead of musing about non-academic matters. I looked down at the sheet, but knew that I wouldn't be able to concentrate. I felt another set of worries rising. "She's being bullied at school," I said.

"Who, Grace?"

"Yes. She's bullied at school and yet she's still so happy about life. I never used to think twice about spending so much time on schoolwork. After all, it's all I really know how to do. But watching her makes me feel like I might be missing out on something."

The confession felt heavy. Likith nodded in response, and was silent for a long while. "I'm not going to lie," he said softly, just as I was about to ask him to say something. "I've thought about how nice it would be to have more time to just enjoy life. But then I think, what if what I'm working towards is something I'd enjoy more than what I could be experiencing now? That's a very likely possibility, Cassidy. And if that's the case, then it's definitely better for me to suck it up and keep on doing what I've been doing."

I looked down at my paper, but once again felt that I wouldn't be able to force myself to think clearly about what was on the page. "I can't stop thinking about it," I said. "Now that I've asked myself all these questions, I can't just un-think them. They're there, begging to be answered, and preventing me from concentrating on anything else." My hands crumpled the top corner of the page. "Maybe we just need to try it once," I said.

"Try what?"

"Try to spend an evening doing something fun without even thinking about work," I said, my voice rising. "It'd be like any scientific experiment. We can test our hypotheses by doing what we've never done before and measuring the results." I felt giddy with excitement as the idea took hold of my imagination. "And then based on those results we can put our questions to rest forever."

Likith smirked, perhaps amused by my excitement. "Do you have in mind a specific way of testing our hypotheses?"

I tried to think of possibilities, but they all involved Grace. My excitement died down as fast as it had come. "Grace mentioned a Fourth of July party and suggested I go, but I got mad because she was trying to take me away from my work, and we yelled at each other and now she's avoiding me," I said all in one breath, embarrassed by the situation's undeniable resemblance to petty teenage drama.

Likith's tiny smirk stretched into a too-big smile. "Of course you would get into a fight about it. You two just can't get along, can you?"

"But we could still go to the party. I think it would be a good test, and probably good for us after these past few weeks." My voice dropped in volume as the thought of how much research I still had to do in the next two weeks popped into my head. Swallowing, I tried to speak again. "I read once that it's really bad to be under lots of stress for long periods of times, because it produces acid that slowly eats away at your muscles."

Likith lifted his eyebrows. "I think that it's a little too late for me to start trying to protect my body from the ravages of stress. And you're probably not any better off," he said, nudging my elbow with his.

"True," I admitted with a smile. "But you like the idea of the experiment?"

Likith returned my smile. "It definitely sounds plausible."

I perked up. "So we're going to the party?"

Likith opened his mouth to respond, but then closed it. I watched the amusement drain from his face. "I can't."

"What?" I whined. "Why? Is it because of the paper?"

"No, Cassidy," he said. "It's my parents," Then he turned back to his worksheet and acted like he was studying it. I, however, wasn't going to let him get away with that vague excuse. I dropped my hand onto the sheet and spread my fingers out to cover most of the text.

"What about your parents?" I asked. "I can assure you that mine wouldn't be thrilled with something like this either. But we shouldn't let that stop us from having some fun now and then."

"No, it's more than that." Likith closed his eyes and sat there as if reading the inside of his eyelids. "When my parents enrolled me in this summer program, it was partly because it would look good on my resume, and partly because they believed I needed to do extra work since my GPA had dropped a bit," he said. He reopened his eyes, and I was alarmed to see that they now glistened slightly. "They said …." He stopped and closed his eyes again, and I recognized that he was collecting his emotions. Then he said in a rush, "They said that if I wasn't perfect in these courses, they were going to send me to India."

"What?" I shrieked. "They're threatening to send you to *India*?"

Likith nodded. "To live with my grandparents and go to school there."

I gaped at him, unable to comprehend why any parent would do that to their child. "They would really give up on you and send you away?" I asked, afraid of the answer.

Likith nodded. "I'd be considered a failure. They would hope that being in India and away from the distractions here would whip me back into shape."

I scoffed. "Like you're out of shape!" Likith looked at me, and his face held so much sadness that I had to divert my eyes. "That is so unfair."

"It really is. It's this horrible double standard. We are never allowed to give up in school, so why should they be allowed to give up on us?"

"Life's unfair," I said with a sigh. I wanted to move on, but was stuck on the concept of Likith being sent to India, ripped away from every other part of his life for the sake of his grades. "I can't believe they would do that," I whispered.

"You should still go to the party," Likith said. "Have some fun."

"No," I said with a shake of my head. "No, I couldn't."

"Okay."

"We're in this together."

"Okay."

Likith smiled and I smiled back, and then we both turned back to our worksheets. I closed my eyes and took a deep breath, letting the oxygen flow to the bottom of my lungs and then out my nose. When I reopened my eyes, they finally cooperated and adjusted to the small print. Relieved that I could finally read my worksheet, I took out a freshly sharpened pencil and began to answer the next question.

chapter 20

Five days after her surprise visit, Mom called to check up on me. "Hi," I said, relieved at the interruption, and gestured for Grace to leave my room. It was the day of the not-on-the-Fourth-of-July Fourth of July party, and Grace had dropped the silent treatment in favor of a last-minute campaign to get me to go to the party with her. "How was your trip home?"

"Good," Mom said. "The traffic was very light. I think I'll use the same route when I come out in a week."

"Right." I swallowed nervously, remembering that I had to prove to her that I was fine staying with the Harpers. "I've made good progress on my paper."

"Oh? What's your topic?"

"It's," I began, then realized how ridiculous 'the physics of refrigerator magnets' might sound to my mother. "I picked one, but I'm still kind of working out the details," I managed.

"Ah," Mom said. I sighed, knowing her one-word answer meant that she wanted to end the conversation or was unhappy with something. And since we had just started talking, I deduced it was the latter.

"You're upset," I stated, sitting down on the bed.

"Well," she began, her voice tight, "I think that if you were working hard and not letting the Harpers distract you, you would have accomplished more by now."

"Mom, it's not due until the twentieth," I said. "I think it'll work out okay."

"Cassidy, you shouldn't wait until the due date to complete an assignment," Mom said. "You know this!"

I back-pedaled. "Mom, I think we've had a slight misunderstanding. That's not what I'm doing."

"Then what *are* you doing?"

"I'm just," I began, but my voice caught in my throat and I had to cough. "I'm trying to enjoy myself a little." I knew it was the completely wrong thing to say, but my mouth was operating independently of my rational brain.

Mom let out a colossal sigh. "Cassidy," she said. "I don't understand what's going through your head right now."

"I'm tired," I said in defeat, letting my mouth take over.

"You can sleep once you finish your paper."

"I don't mean sleep tired, I mean mentally tired!" My voice rose to a yell. "I feel frustrated and burnt out."

Mom sighed again. "Maybe it's because I'm not there," she said. "You used to be so focused on your future, Cassidy."

"Maybe I'm losing sight of it," I mumbled, staring at my free hand. I tried to distract myself by studying the creases of my hand, each line ending at a callus or other writing bruise.

"How can you lose sight of your future?" Mom yelled, and I envisioned her shaking her finger in my face. "It's *your* future!"

Her declaration reminded me of Likith and his future, and how he might be sent to another country just because his grades weren't perfect. The thought made me so mad that my resistance broke. "Is it? Is it really?" I asked, my throat raw. "If it's my future, why didn't I decide any of it? You made all the decisions! I'm just this bundle of neurons whose every action is based solely on the premise that I need to get into a good college to be happy. But I don't know if that's true." I sighed, and thought of Grace using her sighs to blow up the tips of her bangs, just because she could. Grace always did things just because.

"Of course it's true!" Mom said, interrupting my thoughts. "Getting into a good school will pave the way for the rest of your life! It will show people you're smart and have something significant to contribute!"

"But what if there is another way to be significant?" I asked quietly.

"There isn't."

I didn't know how to answer that, so I kept my mouth shut. Mom didn't say anything either. As I listened to the silence, I realized the real question was whether this was the right way to seek significance. Despite what Mom said, I knew there had to be many possible ways, at least as many as there are elements in the periodic table. But somehow this one life-draining method had been labeled as the one-and-only.

"There's a party tonight," I found myself saying, "a Fourth of July party. Grace wants me to go."

Mom remained silent.

"I think I'm going to go."

"Cassidy–"

"No, listen. I think I'm going to go because I don't believe that there is only one way to become significant. I don't know what the other ways are yet, but I know they must exist. And right now, when I'm spending the whole day sitting in a room and working, I'm not going to be able to figure out what those ways are." I paused and breathed in slowly, an unfamiliar emotion mounting in my chest. "At home I never leave the house," I said as I breathed out. "You know why? It's because I'm either working, eating, or sleeping. Eating and sleeping I have to do to stay alive. So that means all the rest of the time, time that should be dedicated to *living,* I spend working. And working is not synonymous with living. Following this to its logical conclusion, as *you* taught me to do, if I want to find out whether there are other paths to significance, I need to leave the house. So that's what I'm going to do. I'm going to deliberately leave the house."

Mom was silent for a long while, except for her mounting breathing. "Cassidy Diamond," she said very slowly, her voice the epitome of sternness, "I am your mother, and even though you are far away right now, I still have the right to parent you. And I say that if you do this, if you go to this party instead of working on your paper, you will be grounded. Not only that, but you will be in *so* much trouble." Mom's voice broke slightly and she stopped. I felt strangely calm. "Is this an attempt to rebel?" she asked after a moment.

I didn't know what an urge to rebel felt like. It was one of the many stages of high school I had skipped, because you don't have time to rebel when you're worrying about maintaining a 4.0 GPA. "I don't know," I said after a while. "I really don't know."

There was another pause. Then, "Cassidy, don't go."

"I'm sorry," I said, alarmed by the anger in her voice.

"Don't go!"

"Mom, I just want to do something social for once."

"Cassidy, I swear–"

never trust a *happy* song

"For God's sake, it's just one night!" I yelled. "It's just one night, and it's not the end of the world. So please calm down."

"You're being irresponsible."

"You know what, maybe so," I said. I stood up and began to pace the room, my anger translating to abundant energy. "I want to go out and talk to people my age, and maybe make a new friend. And if that makes me irresponsible and rebellious, then call me a rebel."

"Cassidy–," Mom began, but I cut her off, tired of her threats.

"I'll talk to you later, Mom." And then I hung up the phone. I had never hung up on Mom before and for a moment I stared at the phone screen, unsure what to do next. Then I threw my phone onto the bed, yanked open the bedroom door, and ran down the hall.

"Grace!" I yelled once I reached the top of the stairs. "Grace!"

"What, what, what?" Grace yelled back. I followed her voice to the dining room table, where she was setting up a trail of dominos.

"I'm going to the party," I declared, my heels bouncing up and down on the floor in exhilaration.

Grace's eyes widened. "What? Really?"

"Yes!"

She giggled, the sound dancing around my already dancing feet. "Cassidy, you're practically jumping. Are you okay?"

"Yes!" I said again, making her laugh harder. But then her eyes narrowed.

"Are you sure?" she asked. "Don't you have to work on your paper or something?"

I shrugged. "I decided one night away from it wasn't going to hurt."

Grace jumped up from her chair. "Really?"

"Yes," I said, grinning. "I figured, you know, seize the day and all that."

"Oh my stars! This is amazing!" Grace ran to me and grabbed my hands. "I'm so excited!"

I jumped up and down with her, struggling to bounce as high in my bare feet as she could in her pink rain boots. The feeling was new, and it made my stomach clench. "When does the party start?"

"In about an hour. Meaning we have to get ready." Grace was singing the words, and as she finished she turned to run up the stairs. My hands were still clasped between hers, but Grace wasn't dragging me this time. My feet danced from step to step, mimicking the movements of a giggling Grace.

chapter *21*

The rush didn't last. Within half an hour I remembered why I didn't go to social events. Three years at a school full of people exactly like me had atrophied my communication skills, rendering me socially awkward at best. As Grace dug through her closet, trying to find something besides overalls for me to wear, my nerves grew. When Grace pulled out a neon green sundress, I began to question why I was doing this.

"How about this?" she asked.

"Um," I tried, "it's kind of bright?"

"True," Grace said, placing her free hand on her hip. "But everything in my wardrobe is bright. Everything that's not overalls or t-shirts, that is."

"Can't I just wear this?" I pleaded, gesturing to my jeans and grey v-neck shirt. I felt comfortable in them, and I wanted Grace to stop fussing over me.

"No," Grace said with a firm shake of her head. "You can't. You will wear this dress."

"Fine," I moaned. "And what are you going to wear?"

Grace turned back to her closet and dug through the rack, pushing a multitude of worn out t-shirts to the side. Eventually she pulled out a hanger with a sundress similar to mine, but hot pink. "This one!" she said, draping the bright fabric over her body.

I found myself smiling, and was thankful for the distraction from how nervous I was. "Of course."

Grace's parents insisted on taking pictures of us before we left, which was incredibly embarrassing. My parents weren't big on photos, so class picture day usually provided most of the camera flashes I had to endure all year. That record was broken by Mrs. Harper, who took a constant stream of photos for what seemed like ten minutes. She kept telling us to change poses and look at each other or pretend to laugh. It seemed pointless to me, and an incredible waste of camera memory, but I reminded myself that I was trying to be more open to illogicality.

The party started at 8 PM, but Grace had us wait until 8:15 to leave. "I've heard it's better not to get to a party right when it starts," she said when I asked for an explanation. "It's called being fashionably late." I noted that this directly contradicted Grace's philosophy of not being fashionable in anything. However, I felt so nervous that I kept my mouth shut, due to fear of throwing up.

"This is going to be so much fun," Grace said excitedly as we sat in the minivan, her feet –for the first time in flats – swinging back and forth.

"I don't know," I said.

"Cassidy Diamond," Grace said, placing her hands on my shoulders and twisting me to face her. "You are not backing out on me, are you?"

"No, no," I fumbled. "I just ...." I looked down and tugged at my lime-green hem. "What if we're wearing the wrong thing and we stand out?"

"Pshaw," Grace said, leaning back in her seat. "Who cares about that? Be comfortable with yourself, remember?" She winked, and I tried to smile, but achieved only a nervous grimace. Pressure rose in

never trust a *happy* song

my stomach, and I looked away, trying to find my bearings. *You can't back out now, Cassidy. If John Brown took the ultimate punishment in silence, then you can get through this.* The pep talk had no effect, and later I wondered if my mistake had been comparing a party to a hanging.

Mr. Harper dropped us off at a square, plain building on the edge of town. The facade was painted two different colors, tan on the left and black on the right. The colors met in a straight line, making the building look like a giant battery.

"Have fun, girls," Mr. Harper said, turning around in his seat to smile at us.

"Thanks, Dad," Grace said as she leaned forward and kissed him on the cheek. "I'll call you when we want to be picked up."

"Not too late, all right?" Mr. Harper looked directly at Grace as he asked this, and for a moment I saw worry on his face.

"Okay," Grace said cheerfully, seemingly unaware of her father's anxiety. She hopped out of the minivan and grabbed my hand, pulling me out the same side.

"Have fun, Cassidy," Mr. Harper said. I opened my mouth to respond, but no words came out. Soon Grace had towed me all the way to the door of the building, and Mr. Harper was gone.

A few feet inside the door sat a girl about our age, positioned behind a desk. Even from afar I could tell she was chewing gum, because she was smacking it loudly between her teeth.

"Five dollars per person," she said in a bored voice.

"I didn't know this was going to cost money," I whispered to Grace.

"Me either," she whispered back. This scared me, because if Grace hadn't known about the entry price, then she hadn't done any research regarding this party. We could be blindsided by other issues we didn't know about. I dug my nails into her wrist. "It's okay," she whispered, placing her hand on top of mine. "I brought money."

I was about to correct her hypothesis regarding the source of my distress, but she gave a ten dollar bill to the girl and once again grabbed my hand, pulling me onward. We headed down a long hall that I assumed would lead to the party room.

"This is so exciting," Grace sang. I wondered if she was aware that she had repeatedly expressed her excitement during the last few hours, so there was no need for her to keep on saying it. I tried to think of an appropriate way to express this, but then my attention was snapped away as I realized how the environment around me had transformed.

As we advanced down the hallway, my ears gradually filled with a solid, undifferentiated mass of noise. The farther we walked, the dimmer the lights became, and my stomach clenched again as I saw that the end of the hall was shrouded in darkness.

"Grace, where are we?" I asked timidly, hoping with all my heart that the noise and darkness weren't a surprise to her.

"The place where the party is being held?" she said, sounding just as timid.

"So why do I feel like we're walking into a person's stomach?"

never trust a *happy* song

"I don't know," Grace said, but she had to yell to compete with the dull roar that pressed against our ears. A few seconds later, we reached our destination, and my tingling intuition that something was off was confirmed.

The room was so dark that I could barely see anything. As my eyes adjusted, I realized that dozens of teenagers were clustered in little groups around the room. Fog spewed from somewhere in the back and slowly oozed toward the front of the room. I felt like I was in one of the cheesy Halloween movies that the little kids I tutor love to talk about.

"Maybe we're in the wrong place?" Grace asked, and as she said it, the truth of the situation hit me with the intensity I associate with finally solving a difficult math problem.

"Grace," I began, grabbing her arm. "You said you got the invitation to this party over e-mail, right?"

"Yes," she replied, and I did my best to remain calm.

"Was it possibly sent by one of those girls?"

"What girls?" Grace asked, but I could tell that her cluelessness was only a pretense.

"What do you mean, 'what girls'?" I shouted, abandoning my resolve to stay calm. "You know exactly which girls I'm talking about!" Grace's eyes, as big and bright as lanterns in the dark and the fog, flitted around the room. "Grace," I said again, tightening my grip on her wrist. "This is a very different kind of party."

chapter 22

Although I had never gone to a "normal" high school, I was aware of the activities that were common at such schools, but didn't exist at mine. Friends from middle school had gone on to those high schools, and although we didn't stay in touch for long, during freshman year they often debriefed me on their party escapades.

I knew of two kinds of parties. A party like the Stanford social night isn't really a party so much as an opportunity to clean up and present yourself to adults. And then there were the high school parties, which more often than not, consisted of sexualized dancing, excessive ingestion of alcohol, and encounters with other recreational drugs. One kind of party had a hidden educational purpose, one was purely social. One kind was merely slightly unpleasant, while the thought of the other made me want to crawl into my bed and hibernate.

Grace and I were definitely at the wrong kind of party.

"Maybe we're at the wrong place," Grace said again, and this time it was less a question and more a statement.

"Grace, we're not," I shouted, taking her by the shoulders. "Dropping the question mark isn't going to make it true!"

"Then what is this?"

"This is the party! A high school party!" I said, giving her a shake with every word. "And I assume that most of these bodies belong to people from your high school."

Grace looked away from me, gazing off into the blackness. When her eyes returned to mine, they were slightly shiny. "So it was a joke," she said, and she sounded so sad that I didn't know how to respond. "They invited me as a joke." I still didn't reply, and she took in a shaky breath. "Grace the Disgrace!" she sneered, mimicking the Mean Girls. "She's such a disgrace to teenagers everywhere, so we're going to invite her to a party full of teenagers so that she can get into her thick head just how much of a disgrace she is!"

Grace was smiling, but the smile looked empty and wrong on her face. She looked away again, shaking her head and breathing in a way that I recognized as an attempt to hold back tears.

I reached for her hand. "We should probably go." Grace snatched her arm back, and I looked up in alarm. Grace, the girl who loved to hold hands, had denied my offer. I realized that she no longer looked like Grace. Her face was hard, with no sign of an impending giggle.

"No," she screamed at me. "You know what, I'll show them."

"Grace, I really don't think that's a good–"

But the Grace I knew was already gone. She turned away from me and stalked off into the crowd, walking with the gait of a person who had snapped. And Grace Harper had most definitely snapped.

I stared after her as she disappeared into the crowd. Then I realized how hard it would be to find her in this large, dark room.

"Wait!" I yelled, though I knew she couldn't hear me. Anyone would have to scream just to be heard by the person standing next to them. "Grace!" I took a deep breath and then ran into the crowd, pushing my way between drunken swayers and grinding couples. My ears were already ringing from the loud music. "Hey!" I yelled, grabbing the shoulders of a tall blond girl. She was dressed like a Mean Girl, so I hoped that she was one. "Have you seen Grace Harper?"

The girl raised her eyebrows and swatted at my hands. "I don't even know who that is!" she shouted. "Who the hell are you?"

"I'm ... my name's Cassidy," I stuttered, not knowing the etiquette for introductions at high school parties.

"Do you go here?" the girl asked, gesturing to the room around us, though it was clearly not the "here" she had in mind.

"No!" I yelled. Then, "What's that smell?"

The girl raised her eyebrows again, and I felt I was being judged. "If you don't know," she said with a laugh, "then I don't think I should tell you."

"That makes no sense!" I shouted, my voice rising in pitch. It had been several minutes since I had seen Grace, and I felt panic burn in my stomach.

The girl raised her eyebrows for the third time, and I wondered if that was the only facial formation she was capable of. "What do you want?" she drawled, apparently already tired of my presence.

"I just want to find my friend!"

"Fine then, go find her!" the girl yelled. "God, aren't you a load of fun." The girl continued her rambling insult, but I couldn't hear her over the music. The song had changed to something even louder, which I would have thought impossible.

"Okay, Cassidy, just look for Grace," I whispered, though I couldn't hear the words. I ran through the list of key characteristics that would help me spot her: tall, thin, short bouncy hair, hot pink sundress. But the room was still darker than midnight and I could barely see my hand held up in front of my face. Spotting anything seemed impossible, even if I did know the identifying characteristics.

never trust a *happy* song

I ventured to the furthest corner of the room, and stumbled upon a large table with an array of cups and bottles. Several people stood around the table, a few looking like they were relying on it for support. I smelled alcohol wafting from them, and backed away reflexively. I must have backed into a group of dancers, because someone grabbed my hips and pulled me to him, and I screamed.

"Don't touch me!" I yelled, whirling around and pushing at whoever it was. He toppled onto the floor, and I ran away.

"Oh God, oh God," I said as I ran to the other corner of the room. If hell existed, I could imagine it being like this, with overwhelming noise and disorienting blackness. Unable to make observations, I could not draw conclusions, and without conclusions I had no idea what to do next. I was tempted to close my eyes and try to calm down by thinking through my favorite math formulas, but I decided that would do little to help the situation. "Breathe, Cassidy," I said. "Go to the last place that you saw Grace and start from there."

I pushed through the crowd again, moving in the direction I believed led to the front of the room. However, when I reached the other side, I found myself in front of the drink table again. I turned around and realized that I had absolutely no idea where I was. I tried to find the place where I had encountered the possible Mean Girl, but either I couldn't find it or she was gone. Out of tactics, I remained where I was, feeling tears in the corners of my eyes.

As I stood trapped, I realized that this was the problem with the real world. In school we are taught to follow things to their logical conclusion, but there isn't always a logical path to follow in the real world. In a math problem, $A = B = C = A$ might hold true, but it will be impossible to prove in the real world. By the time you've worked through A, B, C, and gotten all the way back to A, by then A will have changed. The world isn't static enough for logical conclusions. *So what am I left with?*

I have no idea how long I stood there, watching outlines of people slip by. I lost all sense of time as I tried to think clearly amid the chaos. Eventually a passing shimmer of pink caught my eye. "Grace!" I shouted. "Grace!"

I ran after the pink shadow, and it wasn't hard to catch up with her, since she was stumbling. With both hands, I grabbed her shoulders and turned her around. When I saw it was Grace, I really started to cry.

"Grace! Oh my God, Grace …."

"Cassidy!" she yelled. I moved to hug her at the same time that she exhaled, and I was alarmed by the smell of her breath.

"Ew, Grace," I said, holding her at arm's length. "What did you drink?"

I saw Grace's mouth move, but I couldn't hear her. Everyone in the room was singing along to the music, so it was even louder than before. "What?" I yelled.

"I–" Grace managed, but then another wave of screams hit my eardrums and the rest of her words were lost.

"WHAT?" I screamed, straining my vocal cords.

"I DON'T KNOW," Grace screamed, grabbing my face so that her extra loud scream went right into my ear. "BUT IT CAME IN THESE LITTLE GLASSES, WHICH WERE JUST SO CUTE." I winced, thinking that if my hearing hadn't been damaged already, it certainly was now.

never trust a happy song

"You don't have to yell," I said, shaking her. "How many did you have?"

Grace let out a half hiccup, half giggle. "I don't know. Like seven?" I groaned, and she began to look around the room. "Do you know who any of these people are?"

"No, why should I? They go to *your* school. Now let's go!" Reasoning that we could find the exit by tracing the perimeter of the room, I grabbed Grace's hand and started to drag her toward the nearest wall. Her upper body moved but her feet stayed where they were, so she tumbled onto the floor. I reached down and pulled her to her knees.

"How did that happen?" Grace asked, looking around her as if the darkness held the answer. Meanwhile, I was calculating. *Lack of balance? Check. Alcohol on breath? Check. Confused? Check.*

"Grace," I said slowly, pulling her to her feet. "I think you're drunk."

Grace's forehead wrinkled. "Is that what's making the room spin?"

I closed my eyes, breathing in through my nose and out through my mouth. "Definitely drunk," I muttered to myself. "God, I have no idea how to deal with someone who's drunk." *Okay, Cassidy. Take it one step at a time. First, how to get her home ...*

"Cassidy," Grace whined, tugging on my arm. "I don't know who any of these people are. Why are they all here? I don't want them to be here."

"They go to your high school," I said again, reasoning that staying calm would help this go smoothly. I linked my arm through Grace's to steady her balance.

Grace let out a fake gagging sound. "Ew," she said. Then she ripped her arm from mine and twirled so that she was directly in front of me. "You know, I really hate high school," she yelled, her face inches from mine. "Everything has changed."

"Grace, we need to get you home," I said linking my arm back through hers. "Can you think of anyone who could help you get home?"

"I don't know. Not Monroe, that's for sure. He's too busy ditching me for school stuff. Because school is *so important*." I wanted to say that school *was* important, but I knew this wasn't the right time. Then Grace giggled again. "You know that sound I made earlier, that gagging sound?" She made the noise again, in case I couldn't remember. Then she laughed, big and brash. "That's a funny sound."

"Okay, Grace," I said, pulling her in the direction I hoped led to the door.

"I'm really good at gagging," she said before letting out another half burp-half giggle.

I winced at the mental image. "Grace, you're drunk, all right? Everything you're saying is off-topic and doesn't make sense."

"No, really. You should know, I–" Grace stopped, her hands moving to the sides of her hips. "My hip just vibrated," she said with a giggle. "That feels funny."

"Grace, that's your phone!" I exclaimed. "Give it to me."

Grace fumbled for a moment before reaching underneath her dress and pulling her phone from the waistband of the spandex shorts

never trust a happy song

she wore underneath. She glanced at the screen, her forehead wrinkled. "It's my dad," she said.

"He probably wants us home." I grabbed for the phone, but she held it above my reach. "I'm not sure I can type an answer," she said. "The tips of my fingers feel all numb."

"Then let me do it," I said impatiently.

Grace's eyes lit up. "You would do that? Aw, you're such a great friend!"

I didn't reply as I snatched the phone. The latest message was from Mr. Harper, and read *How's the party going? Just checking up to make sure everything's all right!*

Well, Mr. Harper, I replied in my head. *Everything's peachy. Your daughter is drunk, for starters.*

"Just send my dad a text," Grace slurred. "But make sure it makes sense."

I didn't want to lie to Mr. Harper, but telling him the truth wasn't a great idea either. So I went for option two, and composed a message to Monroe.

Hi, it's Cassidy. Grace got drunk at the party. We need you to help us get home.

It took Monroe two minutes to respond.

GRACE got drunk? As in GRACE HARPER? Are we talking about the same girl?

I rolled my eyes at Monroe's attempt to add humor to the situation, and quickly typed a response.

Yes. Come quickly.

[*175*]

When I looked up to give Grace her phone, she was gone. I almost had a heart attack. "Grace!" I shrieked. "Oh, God, not again."

"Calm down," a voice said behind me. I turned and saw a sober-looking girl, standing with her weight slanted to one hip. "She's over there," the girl said, pointing behind me, "at the drink table." Grace was in fact leaning on the table, looking rather upset. I assumed that by this point she just wanted to go home.

"Thank God," I said, and turned back to the girl. She wasn't the one that I had talked to earlier, but I wasn't sure if she was one of the Mean Girls. She could have been one. They all looked the same, tall and blonde.

"You look like you need a drink," she said.

Her words made me realize how thirsty I was. I wasn't sure that it was socially acceptable to serve water at a party like this. "Yeah, that would be great," I said. "But something non-alcoholic?"

The girl gave me an appraising look before walking to a cooler behind the table. "Sure," she said, reaching inside. She pulled out a bottle, poured its contents into a glass, topped it with a tiny umbrella, and handed it to me. "Here."

"What is this?" I asked, not trusting her. The drink felt very cold and looked as thick as a milkshake.

"It's like a strawberry smoothie," she said as she reached back into the cooler and pulled out another bottle. Hesitantly, I lowered my nose to the edge of the glass and sniffed. *No scent of alcohol*, I recorded. *In fact, it does indeed smell like strawberries. Must be all clear.*

"Thanks," I said, and took a huge gulp.

never trust a *happy* song

I don't remember much else, except that I drank four more smoothies.

chapter 23

It was the umbrella drink that did me in. By the time I realized that they must contain alcohol, my thinking was so impaired that I kept on drinking them. Monroe told me later that when he arrived, Grace and I were stumbling around the room, holding hands and giggling hysterically. I have no memory of that ever happening.

Monroe must have taken us to his house, because the next place I remember being was his kitchen. I was horrified to find myself sitting in a chair while his older sister combed my wet hair. Apparently I had thrown up.

As my thoughts cleared, I realized what an idiot I had been. I should have known not to trust anyone at the party. I should have known not to drink anything. I should have known not to take a drink that had been made by someone else. I should have known something was up after the first sip. *You should have known, you should have known, you should have known.*

"Ugh," Grace said, interrupting my thoughts. "I feel like death."

"Yeah, and you look like it too," Monroe said from somewhere in the room. I heard Grace playfully slap him. Then she added, "Wow. It really was not a good idea to go to that party."

I was tempted to ask at what point it had ever seemed like a good idea. But I realized that I already knew the answer. *Four hours, seven shots, and five smoothies ago.*

"Yeah, not one of your best plans," Monroe said gently. "I think you should stick with the board games." Grace laughed, and I found the strength to lift my head and look at them. Monroe was leaning

never trust a happy song

against the kitchen counter, an odd look on his face. "I'm sorry about the party," he said after a moment. "I'm sorry about, you know."

Grace nodded. "At least I have a story to tell my grandkids when I'm older." She gave Monroe a huge smile, and he smiled back. I didn't smile, and sat there dumbfounded. I couldn't believe it. Grace was letting it go again. Just like that, she was letting it all slide off her shoulders.

"Well, if you're sure," he said.

"I'm sure."

"Well, I'm not," I interjected. They both turned to stare at me as if they were just realizing I was there. "This was possibly the worst experience of my life, okay? I feel awful, I feel stupid, and all because I had to run after you once you decided it was a good idea to 'show them.'" I mimicked Grace's tone, knowing that it was a mean thing to do. But I felt frustrated, and I felt mean. Maybe that's how it felt to be a normal teenager. "That girl," I snarled, "she laced my drink! Why the hell would she *lace my drink*?"

"Oh, I don't know," Grace said, her eyes wild and her voice mean. "Maybe she wanted to tie you up and paint your nails!"

"Or maybe she's evil!"

"Oh really? What on earth gave you that idea?"

I glared at Grace as her sarcasm bit into my skin. "Hey, *you* decided to go with me tonight," Grace said, now almost laughing. "What happened to 'seize the day'?"

"For one, I realized how dumb it was. Second, I realized how dumb social events as a whole are. Third, do *not* blame this all on me. Even if I did make the decision, you know that part of it was your influence. You've spent this entire summer trying to *condition me*, or whatever."

Grace leaned over the back of her chair to push her face toward mine. "Oh, like you haven't tried to change me."

"Not actively, no!" Normally I would feel horribly rude for yelling in someone else's house, but my urge for politeness seemed to have cracked. "I've just complained about your irrationality here and there. But you don't see me sitting you down and forcing you to do your homework!"

"Girls, girls," Monroe said, raising his palms soothingly. "One, you're going to freak out my sister. Two, it's like one in the morning. And three, this is really a pointless argument."

"It's not pointless, Monroe," Grace snapped. She looked at me like she expected a response, but my brain had frozen. Monroe's last statement had reawakened my usual panic.

"He's right," I whispered. I stood up, gripping the back of the chair for support. "No matter what we say to each other right now, nothing has changed. I still am having a fight with my mom, I still have to go to class tomorrow, and I still have to write a paper on stupid refrigerator magnets." My voice broke slightly at the end, and I took in a shaky breath.

My homework. I began compiling a mental list of everything I still had to complete. "Oh, God, I have to go to school tomorrow. I need to get some sleep." But I wasn't going to be able to sleep, because I hadn't finished all my work. And work came first. I had not thought that through when I'd decided to go to the party. I hadn't thought anything through.

never trust a happy song

"Cassidy," Monroe said timidly. "Are you okay?" I realized then that I had begun to cry. I sat back down, my legs feeling shaky.

"I need to go home," I said. "I need to go to Grace's house, please." I tried to make the words sound smooth, but my voice broke as I said Grace's name.

"Okay," Monroe said. "I'll drive you."

"I'm sorry," Grace said. I didn't reply.

And then, because I had turned into a horrible and mean teenager, I said, "You do realize your parents are going to be beyond pissed, right?"

Grace's mouth opened and closed as something, I assumed realization, clicked in her brain. "Oh my God," she whispered. Then she too started to cry.

"Oh my God," Monroe echoed. "I do not know how to handle this many tears."

We sat and cried until Monroe dragged us to his car and drove us home.

I don't remember much about what happened when we got home. I blocked out the details because I wanted to obliterate the whole event from my mind and move on. Grace told me later that it wasn't pretty. We arrived home at two in the morning, and apparently Mr. Harper had been blowing up Grace's phone since ten. I also had a continual string of missed calls from him, starting at midnight. If I had participated in whatever argument took place that night, I would have gently told Mr. Harper that I don't pay much attention to my phone, since only my mother calls me. But instead I held back, not knowing how to approach the issue. Like a coward, I let Grace do the talking, and left Grace alone to face the direct hit of her parents' fire,

Grace was grounded, of course, mostly on the grounds that she scared her parents to death. Grace told them we had both been tricked into drinking, which shocked me because I had never thought of her as someone who would lie to her parents. I was forbidden to leave the house for anything except school, and told that if I didn't behave perfectly they would have to call my parents. This punishment didn't bother me, as it matched my usual routine, and I was thankful that my parents hadn't already been contacted. If keeping this slip-up away from my mom's ears required being grounded, then I was fine with that. The real punishment, in my eyes, was that I didn't start the rest of my homework until 3:30 in the morning.

I can use the trig identities to simplify this equation. On earth we are always falling, since the planets are technically falling, but to us it feels normal. Refrigerator magnets are made with magnetic strips that alternate between attraction towards the north and south poles. $1 + \tan^2 = \sec^2$. If you throw an object at sufficiently high velocity, it will never touch the earth again, and will instead go into orbit. Even though the magnets contain conflicting attractions, they will never scratch the door because they are made from a magnetic powder. Remember that $\cos^2$ is an even function, so if divided by another even function, the result will remain even. Physics, math, physics. Math, physics, math.

I felt like my head was being swirled in a concrete mixer. Too many thoughts fought for my attention, on top of the headache I already had from the night's escapades. *You need to sleep* fought it out with *You need to finish*, and ultimately finishing won because, as Mom would have said, having something incomplete is just as bad as having nothing at all, so you might as well have done nothing. And I wasn't going to let some stupid decision and a spiked strawberry smoothie turn me into a nothing.

So I kept working.

I got maybe two hours of sleep.

chapter 24

Once or twice a year, my school would have a special assembly to talk about the damage that stress and lack of sleep does to teenage bodies. Stress makes our hypothalamus signal our adrenal glands to increase production of two key hormones, adrenaline and cortisol. These hormones raise our heart rate, blood pressure, breathing rate, and metabolism. This increase in hormones allows us to step up to a challenge, such as writing a paper in two hours, playing an important sports game, or getting through a day on low sleep. But if the body turns on this stress response too often or for too long, it causes serious damage. This is called stress overload, and can lead to panic attacks, irritability, headaches, sleeping problems, or even depression. My school always ended this exercise in hypocrisy by saying that if you feel like you are suffering from stress overload, it is very important to step back and take a break.

But you can't take a break. That's not how the school system works.

"You look like hell," Likith said when I entered the lecture hall the next day.

I tried to glare at him, but my facial muscles had a hard time moving. "I didn't really get any sleep," I said, not even bothering to try to think of a witty response. I needed to preserve my brain power for academics.

"Oh, God," Likith said. "Working on your paper?"

never trust a *happy* song

"I wish that was all," I said, burying my head in my hands. I tried not to cry as I listened to the pounding created by every single neuron in my forehead crying out in pain.

"Wait," Likith said after a moment. "Did you go to that party?"

"Yes, and I'd rather not talk about it."

"Oh my God."

"I *said*, I'd rather not talk about it." He held up his hands in a peace offering and rotated his seat to face front.

After a charged pause, Likith spoke again. "I'm sorry you got so little sleep. I've been there, and I know it sucks."

I attempted to smile. "I got all my work done," I said, "and that's all that matters." I struggled to direct my arm down into my backpack to search for a pencil. "Do you know what we're doing today?"

"A demonstration," Likith said. "You could probably sleep through it if you're desperate."

"No," I responded. "I can't afford to miss any information. I need to ace the heck out of this final."

Likith glanced at me sideways, his mouth a taut line. "Me too."

His words brought back the memory of our conversation about his parents, and I shuddered. "I'm sorry," I said. I wanted to say something more meaningful, but it was difficult with my brain screaming *sleep, sleep, sleep.*

I spaced out after that. I might possibly have fallen asleep. All I remember is being catapulted back into reality by Mr. Deal's voice.

"All right, people," he said. "Today is demonstration day. But don't think that means you can slack off. I'll call on people to come up and assist me in solving the physics problems that will be projected on the screen. So you all better be paying attention."

"Likith," I whispered. "Pinch me if I fall asleep."

"You got it," he said with a nod. His mouth turned up in a warm smile that, under different circumstances, would have been extremely comforting. At the moment, it just reminded me that he was able to smile, while I felt like death.

Mr. Deal launched into examples of methods to measure the earth's circumference. While he argued the validity of Eratosthenes's claims, I argued with myself over how I needed to ignore the fact that I was tired and concentrate on the information at hand. *Circular motion. Angle of elevation of the sun and moon. Directly overhead the earth. Measure circumference in–*

Likith pinched me. I whipped my head around to face him, confused because I had been certain I was very awake. "What?" I snapped at him. "Unless I was sleeping with my eyes open–"

"He called on you," Likith whispered back, rolling his eyes towards the front of the room.

I realized the room was completely silent. No sound of Mr. Deal lecturing. No papers being rustled or pencils in use. I slowly turned my head and reluctantly focused on the front of the room. Several pairs of eyes were now centered on me, including those of our professor.

He cleared his throat. "Miss Diamond?"

"Yes?" I asked, trying to keep my voice steady.

"I asked you to please come up and help me determine what Eratosthenes's next step was in discovering the circumference of the earth."

never trust a happy song

"Okay," I responded. I concentrated on keeping my voice steady, while my legs began to shake at the idea of having to stand up. I looked down at them in frustration. *Keep your shit together*, I thought. *Please, just get yourself through the next eight hours.* Then I stood up and walked around Likith to the steps at the end of our row. I directed my gaze toward the front of the room, hoping that, as long as I didn't overthink it, I'd be able to navigate the stairs smoothly.

Mr. Deal cleared his throat again, no doubt frustrated with my slow progress. "So, Cassidy," he said. "How do you think Eratosthenes approached this? He knew the angle of elevation of the sun. He knew the distance from his home city to the sun, and how long it would take for the sun to be directly over the ci–"

That's when his words faded out. I was aware only of the burning in my legs and the pounding in my head as I felt myself fall slowly backwards.

I had never realized how beautiful the ceiling of the lecture hall was. It was slightly rounded, almost like a dome. The plaster was smooth, with no visible cracks, and was painted a light tan. Its shade was different from the color of the walls, but in a way that complemented rather than clashed. Someone must have worked really hard to slowly merge the colors together where the ceiling ended and the walls began. As I stared, it occurred to me that possibly this was the equation for beauty – a creation with differences so subtle that they easily merge together as one. It was a shame, really, because it was so aesthetically pleasing, and yet no one ever looked up at the ceiling.

That was, unless one had just fainted, which I had, and was now lying on the stairs, which I was.

It took a while for my sight and hearing to fully return. Until then, I stared up at the ceiling, gradually becoming aware of a buzz of voices and the sound of my own steady breathing. The latter was a nice reassurance that I was still alive in a world full of people who are constantly dying, even with the scientific theories and medicines that try to keep us alive. But I wasn't dead, as proven by my ability to contemplate the beauty of the ceiling above me. As my senses solidified, I became aware of the shouts of "Cassidy" reverberating above me.

"Cassidy," I heard, "are you all right?"

"Cassidy, can you hear me?"

"Cassidy, drink this water."

"Cassidy, how many fingers am I holding up?"

"Cassidy."

"Cassidy."

"CASSIDY!"

As a pair of hands grabbed my own, I saw a flash of dark skin and knew it was Likith. As he hauled me back to my feet, my voice returned.

"W-what happened?" I asked, though I had a vague idea. But when you regain consciousness, it's best to ask in case something more serious is going on, like a seismic event or nuclear attack.

"You were walking down to the stage when you fell," Likith said, now supporting my back. "Can you stand on your own?"

"Yes, I'm fine," I said, though I still felt shaky.

"Are you all right?" Mr. Deal asked at my side, even though I had just said I was fine.

"Yes, I'm fine," I repeated.

"I'm going to send you home," he said.

"Oh no, really, I'll be fine," I said, trying to stand as tall as possible. "As long as I stay seated and don't do anything incredibly physical, I'll still be able to learn and–"

"Cassidy," Mr. Deal said in the gentlest voice I had ever heard from a teacher. "I want you to go home and lie down." "Okay," I said in a mixture of disappointment and pure joy. *Sleep*, my body cried out. *Sleep, sleep, sleep.*

"Likith," Mr. Deal said. "Please walk Cassidy out to the front entrance. Make sure she doesn't faint on the way there." Likith nodded and Mr. Deal turned back to me. "Call your host family," he said. "Have them pick you up. Then rest for the remainder of the day."

"But what about all the stuff that I'll miss–"

"You can make that up another time," he said with a huge smile, as he was giving me a big present. The reality was that it was simply another death sentence, because the chance was nonexistent of there ever being *another time* when I didn't already have a mountain of work to do. So I would have to cut out even more sleep or meals to finish the work that I would now be missing so that I could sleep and eat.

"Okay," I said, too exhausted to argue. I looked at Likith, and saw that he felt my pain. We shared this sentiment for a moment before he placed his hand on my back and guided me out of the classroom. We walked in silence until we reached the main entrance.

"You okay?" he asked without looking at me.

"I'll be okay," I responded, and he nodded.

"I knew something bad was going to happen the moment you stood up," he said.

"Oh, yeah?"

"Yeah. You just looked so out of it."

"I know. I felt it," I said with a dry laugh. "I felt like I did that one time we had to solve five Reimann sums in one minute and my brain totally shut down."

"Baby, you and I would add up better than a Reimann sum," Likith said with a wink.

"Ugh!" I groaned, and winced. "That was way too creepy. I think Monroe has been rubbing off on you."

He scoffed. "Never!"

"Whatever you say," I sang, and Likith rolled his eyes.

Likith guided me to the row of chairs that lined the wall next to the door. I sat down and zoned out at the feeling of the soft cushion.

"Stay awake," Likith said as I struggled to focus on his face. "Call the Harpers."

"They're going to freak," I groaned, reluctantly pulling out my phone.

"Probably. But they'll also put you in bed and tell you to *sleeeep*," he said.

I smiled. "Sleep does sound good." I stared at my phone for a moment before I remembered how to dial Mr. Harper's number, my fear overpowered by the chant echoing through my head.

Sleep, sleep, sleep.

chapter 25

"You *what?*" Mr. Harper asked a second time, and I could tell that he was struggling to stay calm.

"I fainted in class," I repeated, speaking as articulately as my heavy tongue would allow. "Please don't panic, Mr. Harper. It's not a big deal."

"Not a big deal!" he exclaimed, his volume making me wince.

"Well," I said, "it's a common occurrence at my school." After I spoke the words I realized that, although they were true, they would not calm Mr. Harper down. I smiled as I thought how Mr. Harper would panic if he knew how many kids had fainted in class last year.

"Common occurrence or not, it is definitely cause for concern!" he said. "Are you all right?"

He had already asked this question, and I gave him the same answer. "Yes, I'm fine." *It happened thirty-two times last year, Mr. Harper*, I thought. *Thirty-two times. You would have spent a lot of time worrying.*

"Okay," Mr. Harper said with a deep breath. "I'm going to come pick you up, okay?"

"Yes, please," I said, my head now leaning uncomfortably against the side of my chair. I felt my ability to function slipping away again. It was odd how rapidly my levels of alertness were fluctuating. One moment I could fully engage in a conversation, and the next it was difficult to produce full sentences. "R-really, Mr. Harper," I drawled. "There's no need to worry about me."

"Cassidy," Mr. Harper said, sounding more exasperated. "You shouldn't have fainted. That is a sign that something is wrong. So please don't worry about me worrying about you, and instead worry about being healthy, okay?"

I tried to say 'Okay' back, but I had difficulty opening my mouth. By the time my tongue was prepared to form the required sounds, he had hung up.

"Is he coming?" Likith asked as my hand flopped back down onto the chair.

"Yes," I said softly.

"Good," he said, sounding distant.

"Mhm."

"Cassidy?"

I think I said "Yeah?"

"What happened at the party?"

"I was stupid," I said.

"And what about Grace?"

"She was just Grace."

"What do you mean?" Likith asked.

I meant to reply, but I'm not sure I ever did. The next thing I remember is Mr. Harper picking me up before everything once again turned to black.

I woke up several times over the next few hours, but everything seemed so unreal that I had trouble telling the difference between what was a dream and what wasn't. I think that Mrs. Harper tried to have a conversation with me before I escaped to my bed. I remember her asking the basic questions, like "Are you okay?" and "Why do you think you fainted?" and "Why didn't you get more sleep?"

Grace might have tried to talk to me, but memories of that conversation were interwoven with fantasies of me yelling at her for running off at the party or giving her a huge hug and asking if she was okay. Both were things I wanted to do, but they were way past my comfort zone on the scale of emotional expression. So, if we really did have a conversation, it probably just consisted of her asking me if I was okay, my grumbling that the party was the reason I didn't get enough sleep, and her crying out to her stars.

The problem with being deliriously tired is that even once you're no longer delirious, your body still wants to sleep to compensate for all the stress put on it while you were delirious. As I still had work to complete, that wasn't a privilege I could afford. My poor body, always getting screwed over for my brain.

I reached this point of recovery during the evening. I know it was evening because I woke up to find no light creeping into my room around the sides of the blinds. I tried to be as quiet as possible as I moved around the room, so that I could work in peace for a while before anyone realized I was awake and the worry-fest resumed. Perhaps Grace had her ear pressed to the door, because in less than five minutes I heard a knock.

"Yes?"

"It's Grace," she said. I probably wouldn't have let her in if her voice hadn't sounded so downtrodden.

"Come in," I said with a sigh.

"I know you probably need to work," she began as she opened the door.

I couldn't help laughing. "Really? Since when?" It came out sounding meaner than I had intended, which only made Grace look more like a beaten puppy. "I'm sorry. I didn't mean it like that."

Grace closed her eyes for a long moment. When they opened again, I saw new determination as she danced over to sit on my bed.

"At least you still move the same," I said.

"What?"

"I'd been a little worried about how downtrodden you've looked lately, like someone had kicked you or something." I tried to smile to turn it into a joke, but Grace looked at me stoically.

"Well, I've been sad," she said, looking at me with a directness that made me uncomfortable. "I stupidly decide to go to this party, which I don't know why I did because it's so unlike me. And the party ends up being totally different from what I expected, and I let people pressure me into drinking, which is the complete opposite of everything I stand for—"

"What do you mean?" I interjected. "What do you stand for?"

"Like, being proud of who you are, and of what you do and don't do. Not letting anyone get to you."

I swallowed, my stomach lurching at the thought of the Mean Girls. "I'm sorry about that, by the way." I stumbled over the words, not knowing what I was saying. "I mean, about the invitation and how it wasn't what you thought and—"

"Don't you apologize to me!" Grace said, jumping up so that she was perched on her knees. "I'm the one who took you to a party that ended with us getting home at like two in the morning and then you *fainting*." Her voice caught slightly and she slumped back down into a normal sitting position.

It occurred to me that what Grace was communicating could be guilt. The idea was ridiculous, and that was saying something, considering all the times I'd inwardly blamed her and her antics for keeping me from my work.

"Grace," I said softly, "I *chose* to go to that party. I'm the one who had some sudden brain aneurism and went against everything that *I* stand for."

"But you know I had some influence in it," she said, sounding on the brink of tears. "I had been pushing you so much to branch out or be different, because I hated how you just sat up in this room *working*." Her voice broke again and she paused to take a shaky breath. "I realize now how it was less helping and more me trying to force my beliefs on you."

She started to cry then. I closed my eyes to avoid the sight of tears rolling down her cheeks. I was used to stress tears, like I'm-so-tired-I-have-so-much-work-to-do-the-world-is-overwhelming tears. But these were a different kind of tears, one I didn't know how to handle. "Grace," I whispered, my eyes still closed. "Please stop. There's no need for this."

"I wasn't trying to sabotage you," she said through her sobs. "I hope you know that. I wasn't trying to convince you to change and come to a party just so that you'd be too tired and faint or not have enough time to do well in school. Because I know that's important to you, and I would never try to do that."

"I know," I said softly, daring to open my eyes. She was sitting with her legs pulled to her chest, her cheeks splotchy and red. "I know that, Grace. Please stop crying."

She was quiet for a very long time, and I could tell she was trying to control her tears. "I think they're trying to sabotage me."

Her voice had been so quiet that I almost thought I had imagined it. Then another wave of tears came, but they barely registered, as I was too busy calculating the details of what I had just heard. All of our encounters with the Mean Girls and conversations about Grace's hatred of school replayed in my head. The images mixed together with those of her giggles and smiles, characteristics that I had thought of as indestructible. But there was no trace of either on her face now, and she looked as though she never wanted to smile again.

I realized then that I had been completely wrong about the brain of Grace Harper. She didn't forget events, shaking them away in order to be happy. She kept track of them just as well as I had, forming them into her own list of reasons why she *needed* to be happy.

"Are you okay?" I whispered, posing the question that everyone had been irrationally asking me. It was obvious now that the person who really needed to be asked was Grace.

"I don't know," she said. I just nodded and cleared my throat. "Are you?" she asked, unfolding herself from her curled position. "Oh my stars, Cassidy, all I can think about right now is how you *fainted*–"

"Stop saying it that way," I interjected, reaching out to touch her shoulder. "Stop saying the word like it's such a horrible thing. I just didn't have enough sleep, that's all. I just pushed my body a little farther than it was willing to go, and fainting was its way of telling me."

never trust a *happy* song

"Your body was telling you that it was sick!" she yelled. "You should have listened to that and *not gone to school.*" She slapped the bed between every word of the last phrase, making it very clear that she disapproved of my decision.

I paused for a moment, searching for the right words, but failed to come up with anything to defend the habit that was like breathing to me. "No," I said defensively.

Grace pursed her lips. "But why?" she said, dragging out the word in exasperation.

"Because I'm not going to let life take my hard work away from me. I'm not going to let it defeat me." I said. As the words slowly came to me my voice became more adamant. "Skipping school just because I feel bad would be like giving up. Sickness is just something that tries to prevent us from succeeding."

"That makes no sense!" Grace practically screamed. I hushed her in a panic, not wanting to catch the attention of her parents. "That makes no sense," she repeated in a broken whisper that matched the defeat in her eyes.

"Think of it like this," I said. "We live in a society where there is an expectation that in order to be successful, you must go to a prestigious college." I caught the flash in Grace's eye before it could be translated to her mouth. "And it may not be the only route to success," I said, holding up a finger, "but that attitude has conquered the minds of many parents and teenagers. So, all these kids are frantic to get into these schools that expect their students to be smart, creative, hard-working, and studious. But that's not enough to get admitted. To get in, you have to be all that and still manage to have some aspect of your life that sets you apart, makes you significant. A really special student is someone who has won a national science competition, is nationally ranked in swimming, or has a painting on exhibit in New York City. We are expected to be like that, and maybe it's crazy and wrong and damaging, but that doesn't change the fact that the expectation exists. And the bar has to be that high, because otherwise everyone would be getting into these schools. The system is purposely set up so that many will fail. It is expected that many will sink under the combined pressure of school, and extracurricular activities, and the need to sleep. And I refuse to sink."

I sucked in air, shocked that Grace had allowed me to go on for so long. She was staring at me, her eyes as wide as always, her brown hair brushing the straps of her overalls as she slowly shifted back and forth. In this rare quiet moment I found myself once again observing Grace, analyzing her piece by piece. Every part of her seemed coated with a thin layer of depression. I tried to remember how perky and bright Grace had been when I'd met her only a month and a half earlier. It was hard for me to superimpose those images onto the person before me. I wondered if she looked so desolate now just because she was sad, or if something deeper in her chemical makeup had changed.

"Isn't that scary?" she said eventually. "Isn't it scary to have to deal with all of that at once?"

"Well, yeah," I said, forcing my attention away from the questions and doubts that constantly circled in the fishbowl of that was my mind. "But what's the use of being scared?"

"Sometimes it helps you do things," she said quietly.

"Like what?"

never trust a *happy* song

She cleared her throat. "Sometimes being afraid actually helps people get through life. It propels them, like adrenaline."

I stared at her a moment, her eyes so big that I felt like they could swallow me up. "Grace, that's completely irrational. I mean, maybe that can work some of the time, but then what do you do when you become too scared? Too scared to live, too scared to die, too scared to even care?"

"Is that possible?" she asked, her voice very quiet now.

"Yes."

"What happens then?"

"Well, I guess eventually those people will die."

Grace was very quiet and very, very pale. She looked almost inhuman now, her hair thin and stringy around her hollow cheeks. "I'm scared," she whispered.

"Why?"

"Because I always say that my one goal is to make sure that I am comfortable with myself. And I used to not even have to think about it, but now every day it seems to get harder." Grace shifted on the bed, bringing her feet up in a clumsy movement, but they slipped down again. Grace took in a shaky breath, and I looked down to see that her rain boot had left a dirt smudge on the edge of my blanket. Grace began to scrub at it, her fingers plastered together. "And, I *say* that I'm being myself," Grace continued as she focused on the stain. "I say it all the time! But sometimes I'm not even sure I have a self to be comfortable with."

"That's not true."

"Yes, it is."

natalie bina

"No, Grace–"

"And something else!" Grace was almost shouting now, and she turned to point her now dirt-stained fingers at me. "I don't know what I want in life! And...." Grace seemed to struggle with the words, and all of a sudden her body became very still. "And you do. And that scares me. Because I don't even know what I want right now."

"That doesn't mean that there's anything wrong with you! That's perfectly normal!" I said, reaching out to touch her. She jerked away, and now I felt scared. The Grace I knew seemed to be draining away, leaving behind some stoic person with no passions of any kind, just worries and fears. *A heart valve draining its fluid, John Brown walking towards his noose,* I thought. And then, a question: *Did I do this to her?*

I reached forward again, and this time grabbed her hand before she could jerk away. "Grace," I said gently, "are you okay?"

"I need to go to the bathroom," she said. My brain stalled, not knowing how to move forward.

"Well, okay."

"I need to go," she said, as if I was holding her back. But she could easily pull her fingers out of my hand. Nothing was keeping her on the bed.

"Okay." I wanted to slap myself for saying the word as soon as it was out, because that had been my opportunity to keep her attention and I had missed it. "Grace, wait!" I yelled, but it was too late, because she had already slipped out of my grip and slammed the door behind her. I sat there, frozen, for who knows how long, listening to the silence and, after a few minutes, the sound of running water.

Eventually someone entered my room, but it was Mrs. Harper. I slowly turned my head and gazed at her. She really did look like an adult version of Grace. Her physical qualities were almost identical.

"Have you seen Grace?" she asked.

"I think she's taking a shower," I said, almost robotically. "At least, I hear the water running."

"Huh," Mrs. Harper said. "That's odd. She took one earlier today."

I shrugged. "Maybe she likes to think in there. It's not unheard of. I once read a study about the positive effects of water on the brain."

This brought a smile to Mrs. Harper's face. "Oh, Cassidy," she said, "you really are something. So smart." She patted me on the head before walking out the door.

I continued to listen to the running water until sleep grabbed hold of me, dragging me away from consciousness.

chapter 26

On the morning of the day that I saved Grace's life, I came downstairs to find her already eating breakfast at the dining table. She was wearing the same superhero t-shirt she had worn on the day I met her. The shirt still had the same stain, a spot of darkness that matched the heavy circles underneath Grace's eyes.

Grace didn't notice my arrival, and I felt awkward standing there as she chowed down forkfuls of food. I quietly cleared my throat, and Grace whipped her head around to stare at me, her eyes wide.

"You must be hungry," I said after she continued to stare, thinking that maybe she expected me to say something. Grace just nodded, then returned to her plate. "Are you mad at me?" I asked after a moment of listening to her chewing. Her head whipped back around.

"No," she said, her chipper voice sounding odd compared to the fatigue I could see in her eyes. "Why would I be?"

"I don't know. We had that conversation last night and now...." My jaw opened and closed a couple of times, my speech halting. "I'm not very good at this," I said with a sigh.

Grace smiled slightly. "I know." I moved to sit next to her at the table, placing several web page printouts next to her plate. "What is that?" she asked.

"Research for my paper."

"About refrigerator magnets?" Grace asked with a grin.

"Yes." Then I couldn't help smiling as well. "God, it sounds so ridiculous."

"I think it's great! Good for you, researching something as underappreciated as refrigerator magnets."

"Oh yes, because they bring so much joy to people's lives."

Grace tilted her head, her bright eyes still on me. "They do."

After that we sat in silence, me reading while Grace ate. It was a funny moment, I realized, as we had never before been in such harmony. When I started high school, Mom had warned me that I would dislike ninety percent of the people there. This had baffled me, because I couldn't imagine how I could work alongside someone I disliked. I didn't hate Grace, but I knew I wouldn't want to be around her all the time. And yet here we were, willingly sitting in comfortable silence. It seemed illogical, and yet I knew the world was made up of opposites. Wet and dry, hot and cold. To say they worked together in perfect harmony would be a lie, but to say we could exist without them would be underestimating their importance. *So maybe Grace really is important to me*, I thought. And then, *Will it be weird when she's no longer around?*

Grace had long finished her food by the time Mr. and Mrs. Harper descended the stairs. I had gotten up incredibly early because I'd slept most of Friday, so I assumed it was now normal breakfast time.

"Who's ready for some pancakes?" Mr. Harper asked, confirming my hypothesis.

"Oh, me," Mrs. Harper said with a yawn, half-raising her hand.

Mr. Harper cocked a grin. "Well, then you'll have to make them."

The entire Harper family burst into laughter, and I felt like the room was being bombarded with shots of giggle hormone. But I couldn't deny it was contagious, for soon I found myself laughing with them.

"All right, girls," Mrs. Harper said after she had recovered. "Breakfast will be ready soon." She walked towards us and rested her hands on our shoulders. "You two didn't eat dinner last night. You must be hungry."

"That's for sure," Grace said, licking her lips in exaggerated anticipation.

"But what about–" I began, but her plate was gone. Grace continued to lick her lips and Mrs. Harper laughed, so I just closed my mouth as Mrs. Harper retreated into the kitchen.

"How was your Friday evening, Grace?" Mr. Harper asked. Foreseeing another chit-chat filled conversation, I returned to my research. *Refrigerator magnets alternate between attraction and repulsion.*

"It was okay. It kind of sucked that I didn't get to go bowling with Monroe, though."

It is possible to do tests that show how a certain magnet's strips are arranged.

"Well, yes, that's unfortunate. But that's because you're grounded."

"I know."

The oppositely polarized strips attract each other.

"You'll be ungrounded in a week."

"Okay."

This means lining them up causes the two oppositely polarized magnets to stick together.

never trust a happy song

"You know I'm not the kind of teenager who's going to party, right?" Grace asked suddenly, breaking the short silence that had allowed me to come up with that discovery.

"I don't know that for sure."

"Dad! What have I ever done to make you think that, other than that one incident?"

This structure allows the magnet to be maximally attached to the refrigerator door.

"Well, nothing. It's just that one incident that worries me."

"Trust me, Dad. There's no reason to worry. That was just stupid girls being stupid." Despite my efforts to tune it out, I heard this part of the conversation. My throat inexplicably tightened at the mention of the Mean Girls, and I gripped my pencil.

This is done by...by...

"As in you being stupid?"

"Da-ad," Grace whined, and she now had my full attention, though I kept my eyes on the papers.

"Well, it was!"

"And I know that. I was just talking about *other* girls."

"What other girls?"

There was a substantial pause in the conversation as Grace began to tap her finger on the table, setting an erratic offbeat rhythm. As much as I wanted to wait for her to continue, my annoyance forced me to intervene.

"Grace, stop tapping," I hissed.

"Sorry," she said, tugging at the sleeves of her t-shirt. "Cassidy's studying, Dad. We can finish talking about this later."

"Talking about what?" Mrs. Harper interjected as she walked into the room with a plateful of pancakes. I remembered I was starving as soon as their aroma reached my nose.

"Nothing important, Mom," Grace said, moving two pancakes to her own plate.

"No, it was important," Mr. Harper said. "It was about some girls at that party."

"Oh." Mrs. Harper's mouth formed a straight line, a rare absence of her usual smile. "What happened, Grace?"

"It's nothing. Some girls who are kind of mean were kind of annoying at the party," Grace said, rushing the words. "But I'm kind of hungry now. So could we *please* talk about this later?"

"That was a lot of 'kind of's," I said with a smile.

Grace turned to glare at me. "Ha, ha."

"My, my, aren't we irritable this morning," Mrs. Harper said, looking a bit hurt.

Grace froze, and I wondered if she was going back over everything she had just said. I watched as her features softened. "You're right. I'm sorry. I'm just tired."

"We all get a little tired sometimes, sweetheart," Mr. Harper said. Then he gave me a little smile. "Just don't get so tired that you faint." I forced a smile in return, knowing that was what he wanted, even though I found no humor in the sentiment.

The Harpers dug into their food. Grace did so with as much fervor as her parents, even though she had already eaten a meal. I found this curious because I didn't think of Grace as having a large appetite – not that I paid much attention to people's eating patterns.

Without realizing it, I had been staring at Grace, and she turned to stare back at me. "Cassidy, are you analyzing me or something?" she asked, and I couldn't tell if her voice contained humor or irritation.

"Maybe."

"Oh my stars!" she exclaimed loudly, her disposition now clear. "What *is* it with everyone this morning?"

"What do you mean?" Mrs. Harper asked, setting down her fork.

"Here I am, getting all the questions and attention, when *Cassidy*'s the one who fainted yesterday!"

"Grace, why are you making a fuss?" Mrs. Harper's voice had risen in pitch, indicating that she was now clearly irritated. "We were just discussing things. That's all."

Grace opened and closed her mouth several times before visibly deflating, sliding down in her chair. "I'm sorry," she said almost inaudibly. "Can I be excused?"

Mrs. Harper gave her husband a worried glance. "If you really want to be," she said after a moment.

"Yes. I think I need to go upstairs," Grace said, slowly scooting her chair back. I stared at her pale face as she moved her chair.

"But what about your food?" Mr. Harper asked, pointing at her plate. "You said you were starving."

"I'm full now," Grace said quietly, and then she turned and ran up the stairs. The three of us sat in silence, and I found that my hunger had left me as well.

Mr. Harper sighed and pushed his plate away. I kept my eyes straight forward, as I didn't want to see the Harper's faces, which no doubt displayed a combination of fear, frustration, and confusion at the odd way that their daughter was behaving. I was feeling many of the same emotions, but one other as well: hot, uncomfortable guilt. The guilt brought a new thought into my mind: *Do Mr. and Mrs. Harper see that Grace only started acting differently after I moved in? Do they blame all of this on me?* The burn grew as events and comments that I had witnessed over the past few months clicked into place, producing a scorchingly bright conclusion. My mouth went very dry.

    I didn't realize I was standing up until I felt my knees straighten. "Could I be excused as well?" I asked shakily.

    "Yes, of course," Mrs. Harper said after a moment. "You should get some more rest."

    I nodded, the whirring in my head overpowering any possibility of speech. I walked up the stairs robotically, knowing that I had caught onto something, but not exactly sure what it was and seeking relief from the fire inside my head. On the way to my room, I noticed that Grace was in the bathroom again.

    "Grace?" I asked, knocking on the door. "Are you okay?" There was no response. The water was running. "Grace?" I asked again.

    After listening to the tinkling of the water for a few more moments, I gave up and started to pace. My feet moved of their own accord, and even though I knew it was wrong, I found myself heading for Grace's room. I had never once been in her room, perhaps due to the irritation I felt every time she came into mine. As I slowly opened the door, the first thing I saw was her bed, pushed up against the opposite wall. Her bedspread had the same superhero faces that I recognized from her t-shirts. I half-heartedly wondered if she knew whether her bedspread was washable, while the other half of me thought about the water.

Water. Running water. Why would someone always run the water? To take long showers? To thoroughly wash their hands?

Grace had a bulletin board next to her bed. It was similar to the one in my room, only mine was empty, and Grace's board was plastered with notes and photographs. Most of the photos showed just Grace, smiling brightly in overalls and a t-shirt. There were a few of Monroe, and several of her parents, but it was mostly a multitude of Graces, all looking equally happy. The top left corner of the board held a messy stack of neon-colored sticky notes. I knew it was wrong to look, even more wrong than being in her room, but I found myself drifting closer to the board and the answers it might hold.

Why so much water? She could be a germophobe. But she always wears dirty rain boots in the house…

As I grappled with my inability to derive an explanation, I could hear Mom's voice scolding me for being such a snoop. As I got closer and closer to the vibrantly colored notes, the lecture increased in volume.

Life is like a song, the first note read.

No, Cassidy, life is like a homework assignment, my mother's voice said. *You must finish it, no matter what.* I violently flipped to the next note, as if the action would silence the words.

Reach for the stars, the next one said, and as I read it I could imagine Grace muttering, "Oh my stars," with a roll of her eyes. I flipped to the next note, and the next. Each one contained an inspirational note or therapeutic statement. They were all incredibly upbeat, almost nauseatingly so. Before I could even register how many I'd gone through, I reached the bottom of the pile. The last note was different from all of the rest. Instead of a sentence, it just had one word on it: *eat*. The word was written in all capital letters, and had been underlined three times. *EAT*.

All the pieces clicked together, as though I had finally solved a math puzzle I had known the answer to all along.

"Grace," I called out as my pulse rose and I headed for the door. "Grace! Grace!"

I ran down the hall to the bathroom, mentally reviewing all the times I'd seen Grace eat plenty of food, versus all the times I'd seen her eat nothing, versus all the times she had locked herself in the bathroom with the water running. The thought that I was crazy and overreacting was overlaid with the image of Grace spending hours sitting in front of a refrigerator that I'd never seen her actually open.

"Grace!" I yelled again, my voice rising to a scream. "Grace, I need to get in there. I, uh, I need to borrow a toothbrush!" I pushed my ear even closer to the door, and maybe I was just imagining it, but I thought that I heard her over the sound of the falling water. I pounded my fists on the door, the rhythm reminding me of her humming and skipping. It was so pathetic, I thought, that I had no idea how to stop her. All that came to mind were facts about electrolyte levels and how imbalance could stop nerves, muscles, and even organs from functioning correctly. But as long as I was on the wrong side of the door, those facts did no good.

"Grace, I'm coming in!" I yelled, and began to hurl my body against the door, trying to force it open. My pounding and screaming must have brought Mr. and Mrs. Harper up the stairs. Next thing I knew, Mrs. Harper had pulled me back and was hugging me to her chest while Mr. Harper kicked in the bathroom door. The splintering of the door jamb sounded in harmony with Grace's scream.

chapter 27

Bulimia nervosa is a sickness with many complications. The first side effect is dehydration from constant loss of fluids and nutrients. This can be combated by drinking lots of water, but it still often causes long term damage. Repeated self-induced vomiting can tear the esophagus, which in turn can lead to coughing up blood. Acid reflex, anemia, pancreatitis, and kidney infection are the more intense complications, which often lead to death. Of course, as I inferred from the online textbook on eating disorders that I pulled up on my phone, most bulimics won't suffer from the more extreme complications until they've been purging for a year or so. The doctors guessed that Grace had only been bulimic for a few months. Still, that didn't make me feel any better.

Worse than my own distress was having to sit in the waiting room with Mr. and Mrs. Harper, while Grace was hooked up to a tube that would feed her nutrients. We sat in silence, Mr. and Mrs. Harper staring straight ahead while I studied the patterns in the carpeting. The weaving had produced a pattern of boxes, which reminded me of a large but empty table of data, begging to be filled with information. Sitting in silence, I began to fill it in.

Sometimes people just fall apart – I knew that. I had spent the last two years watching people around me collapse under the stress of school. But Grace's falling apart had blindsided me; it was an effect that I was unable to link to its cause. As I mentally added this information to the table, I thought back on all the times that Grace had said she was scared. Now, I wondered what it was that she had been more afraid of: her future or her falling. I stared at the squares and tried to make sense of the evidence, until I could bear the silence no longer.

"I'm sorry," I blurted.

"Why?" Mr. Harper said sharply, leaning forward. "Did you do something?"

"No. At least, I don't think so."

"Then why did you say you were sorry?"

I faltered, not used to hearing such a harsh tone from anyone other than a teacher or my mother. "I don't know. I...I'm not very good at this. I never know what to say."

"Well then don't say anything," Mr. Harper bit out, and I felt tears come to my eyes. "No, *I'm* sorry," he said a moment later. "That was uncalled for." I looked up and watched as Mr. Harper ran a hand through his thinning hair. "I'm just so confused. I saw no warning signs for this. This just isn't like Grace."

"I know."

"I thought she was happy."

"I know," I said slowly, my tongue heavy.

"At least, she always *seemed* so happy. Didn't she?" Mr. Harper turned to Mrs. Harper, who had been sitting very still.

"Yes," she responded slowly. "She's always skipping around and humming that happy tune."

"But that doesn't necessarily mean she was happy," I said, looking at nothing in particular.

"What do you mean?"

"Just because she was always singing a happy song doesn't mean she was happy. That's not a guarantee. I mean, a song on the radio might sound happy, but then if you listen to the lyrics it could turn out to be the saddest song in the world. Certainty in music can't be assumed. You should never trust a happy song."

Mr. and Mrs. Harper exchanged a worried glance before turning their attention to me. "Well, Cassidy," Mr. Harper said after a moment, "then what can we trust?"

"I don't know," I breathed out. "Facts. Science, math. Things that are concrete."

"I never had reason to look for something more concrete," Mrs. Harper said quietly. "And she was always having fun...." She trailed off, her words so quiet that I suspected they were no longer meant for me. "No matter what she did, she always had so much fun. I never worried about her, because she just seemed so content." Mrs. Harper looked very sad then, and I looked down, not wanting to intrude. "Maybe we did something wrong," I heard her say after a moment.

"No." The word was out of my mouth before I could even think about it.

"Maybe we should have pushed her more. Maybe, instead of being content with where she was, I should have pushed her to do better in school, make more friends, and study harder for tests–"

"No."

"–I mean, that's what your mother did, right? She pushed academics. And look at you! You're happy, and you're okay–"

"No!" I accidentally yelled it, and several people in the waiting room turned to look at me. But in that moment I didn't care, *couldn't* care. "No, that is not true. I am *not* okay."

never trust a *happy* song

"You're not in the hospital!" Mr. Harper said, lowering his voice to a harsh whisper. "You don't have the problems Grace has!"

"But I have my own problems!" I said, and although it couldn't be heard in my voice, I knew I was crying. "Mr. and Mrs. Harper," I said softly, "I am *not* okay. Maybe you're right. Maybe Grace wasn't pushed hard enough. But I have been pushed too hard. And I am *not* okay."

I must have really begun to cry, because Mrs. Harper stood up and walked over to my chair, giving me a small hug. "I think I need to call my mom," I said softly.

"All right," Mrs. Harper said. And then, "Oh no! I never told your mother about you fainting! I meant to call her this morning, but then there was all the trouble with Grace...."

"That's fine," I said, and I couldn't help the smile that spread across my face when I thought of how un-newsworthy my mom would find that tidbit. "I'll do it."

"Okay."

I tried to smile at both of them before I stood up, realizing how much I would miss them. I would miss their kind faces and their overreactions, and the odd ways in which they were simply parents. My hand trembled as I started the call to Mom and held the phone up to my ear.

"Mhm?" she answered, her voice broken up by the crackling of a weak signal.

"Mom?" I said. "Where are you?"

"I'm driving through the Sierras."

"Through the Sierras? Why?"

"I'm coming to visit you, honey!" she said.

"Oh my God," I replied, realizing that I had completely forgotten about my two-week-long second chance. My time was up.

Mom laughed in response. "So I'm guessing you've been so caught up with work that time just passed you by?"

"Um, yeah," I said, trying to piece together my next few sentences as I paced the periphery of the waiting room.

"Cassidy, what's wrong?" Mom asked, ever the wizard at detecting distress in my voice.

"I fainted in school," I blurted, completely without a plan. "And Grace has bulimia."

"I'm sorry to hear that," Mom said. Then, "So I should start looking for a replacement host family, then?"

"What? No!" I exclaimed. "That's not the point!"

"I'm extremely sorry to hear that Grace is suffering from an eating disorder, but that is not something you should have to deal with while you're finishing up this summer term. I know you have a big paper due soon."

"Yes," I said, not even bothering to ask how she knew that.

"What are you writing about?"

"Refrigerator magnets."

There was a long period of silence. "*Refrigerator* magnets?"

"Yes."

I heard her breath quicken. "May I ask *why*?"

"Because they're interesting."

"That's not interesting, it's ridiculous!" my mom yelled. "That girl gave you that idea, didn't she?"

"Yes," I said, even though I could have easily lied and perhaps stopped the whole argument there. "She did."

"I'm getting you a new host family."

"No. No, you're not," I said, my voice shaking. I wasn't an arguer, and I certainly wasn't a confronter, but the thought of Grace alone in a hospital bed with a tube down her throat made me incredibly angry. "And Mom, I'm not retaking the SAT IIs."

"*What?*" she snapped.

"Mom, I got an 800!" I yelled. "I don't think I should have to retake it!"

"You got an 800 when you were a *sophomore*," my mom stressed. "Now you need to prove to colleges that you can still get that score as a *junior*."

"I shouldn't have to prove anything!"

"The road is getting twisty, so I need to hang up to focus on driving. I'll be in Palo Alto soon, and then we'll figure this all out," she said, the calm returning now that she had decided to ignore me.

"Mom, I'm *sick*." I struggled to get the words out through my tears. "I am not okay. I am so unhappy…I just want to be happy."

"We'll figure this all out, and you're going to get into your dream college, and you're going to be happy."

"I–" But, just like always, Mom hung up. But unlike all those other times, I was crying, and I was standing in a public place, and two adults were rushing over to lead me back to my chair.

"It's going to be okay, Cassidy," Mrs. Harper said as she wiped her finger underneath my eyes.

"I just talked to the doctor, and he said that Grace is going to be just fine."

"But what about her electrolyte imbalance?" I blurted through my tears. Mr. Harper chuckled. "I'm not sure about that, but I know that he said there was no permanent physical damage. We'll be able to go talk to her soon."

"So no esophagus ruptures?"

"No."

"No kidney infection? Anemia?"

"Uh, no–"

"What about pancreatitis? Because I read that–"

"My God, Cassidy," Mrs. Harper cut in. "Did you research this?"

I wanted to laugh, but instead I just kept crying. Mrs. Harper pulled me into a hug, and I stayed in her arms until a doctor came and told us that Grace was allowed to have visitors.

chapter 28

"Why do you do it?"

I was sure it wasn't the nicest thing to say, or even the best thing to say, but I couldn't think about anything else. I had waited for an agonizingly long time as Grace's parents spoke to her alone, the question brewing in my head until it was finally my turn to enter her room. I examined the way that she was wrapped up in blankets, her back propped up by pillows, and wondered if she was really as okay as the doctors said she was.

"Do what?"

"You know what," I said, advancing to the side of her bed. "Why do you do it?"

Grace was quiet for a long time. "You mean make myself throw up?"

Her voice was so quiet that I almost didn't hear it. "Yeah," I muttered. "That." I sensed that Grace was going to shrug, and kept talking to postpone her non-answer. "I mean, you're not overweight. *Please* tell me you know that you are not overweight."

"I know that I'm not overweight."

"Well then, what is the issue?"

"Can you really not see it? You of all people?"

"See what?" I exclaimed. My hands were now gripping the side of her bed, and I leaned over the bed rail so that I could focus on her face.

"I have no purpose!" Grace said, staring up at the ceiling. "No control! I have no goal that's driving me forward. I just la-di-da through life like I have nothing to worry about, when really I have lots to worry about, and many of them are things that I should've started to worry about a long time ago."

"Grace–"

"And how am I going to be able to handle the future when I can't even handle high school? I mean, I don't fit in. You know that. I'm not smart. You know that too."

"Grace–"

But Grace intercepted my words, no doubt knowing what I was going to say. "Shut it, Cassidy. I get C's and B's. I'm not smart."

I didn't know how to respond to that. I didn't even know that I was going to respond until the words tumbled out of my mouth. "Grades aren't everything. They aren't the say-all-end-all way to define intelligence. In the time I've been here, you have said and done things that show you have way more smarts than most people do." I had never contemplated that thought before, yet here it was, articulated as clearly as if I had known it for years. My spontaneity caught me so off guard that I was startled into silence for a few minutes. Grace spent that time staring at the ceiling. "Maybe the problem with your grades means that you need to do a better job of applying yourself?" I offered eventually.

"Fine, then. I can't apply myself."

"That's not what I–"

"Please stop trying to make me feel better, Cassidy! My stars," she muttered, still not looking at me. "You're so blatant about your own issues and yet you won't even accept mine."

"I don't understand."

"I'm *weird*, Cassidy. I know you see it! I'm weird and people tend to not like me. I'm awkward and I like to skip and sing and I don't care about my clothes or how I look."

"So?" I said quietly. "That's what makes you unique. All that stuff sets you apart from everyone else, makes you stand out."

"What's so great about standing out if it means no one likes you?"

I felt like someone was squeezing my heart. "People do like you. *I* like you."

Grace let out her breath all at once, and it sounded like helium draining out of a balloon. "You still didn't answer my question," I said as gently as I could. "Why do you do it?"

After a lengthy silence, Grace finally looked at me. "I was scared."

I smiled gently. "I know that."

Grace continued as though she hadn't heard me. "I mean, *really* scared, Cassidy. Scared I wasn't going to go anywhere, or be anything."

"You will."

"Please."

"You'll be Grace Harper, the girl who sings happy songs and loves to make sentences with refrigerator magnets and makes people laugh."

Grace smiled and rolled her eyes, and I couldn't tell if it was because she liked that idea or because she thought I was being ridiculous. Either way, she eventually started to laugh. It sounded more subdued than normal, but I still couldn't help but laugh along with her. "See?" I said through my giggles. "And you've already done something for me."

"Oh?"

I nodded. "Maybe you're right. I shouldn't spend so much time on homework or studying. I mean, I still think it's important to get it all done, but...." I trailed off, and Grace looked at me with shining eyes, clearly pleased that I was about to admit she was right. "*Maybe* it's also just as important to make sure I sleep and, you know, actually have fun sometimes."

Grace grinned at me. As I looked at her, I once again noticed how dry and patchy her skin had become since I'd first met her. Where her cheeks used to be smooth and shiny, her grin now pulled lines into dry skin. "Cassidy having fun," she said, her voice full of wonder. "Imagine that."

"Yeah," I replied. And then, with a huge lump in my throat, "And maybe if I hadn't been so caught up in all those things, I would have noticed what you were going through. Maybe I would have noticed that there was a really serious issue."

"Don't worry about it," Grace said, looking away.

"I can't help it. I feel guilty," I said, my words overlapping hers. "You don't need to be scared, Grace. Trust me, I understand. The future is *terrifying*. I spend all this time working to prove that I'm smart and can get into a good college that will pave the way for my future, but I have absolutely no clue what I'm going to do once I get there! But that doesn't mean that I should stop living now." I nudged her arm with my fist. "I refuse to sink, remember?"

Grace gave me a little smile. "Those girls at school just made me feel like crap. I used to know how to be myself and then it was like they took all of that away. And with just one little look or word...."

Grace bit her lip and looked down, her hair falling into her face. "God. I just felt so dumb."

I clenched my fist, the idea of the Mean Girls making me so frustrated. "When I first met those girls, I had no idea why they went out of their way to treat you the way they did. It baffled me. But now I think…." Grace looked at me as I trailed off, and I resisted the urge to look away. "Now I think that they're just scared too."

"Scared of what?" Grace spat, her face now the epitome of all that I thought wasn't Grace.

"That you know something that they don't."

"Please," Grace said, rolling her eyes, "I don't know anything. I don't even know how to control my eating anymore," she said, plucking at one of the tubes connected to her body.

"You need to stop that binge and purge routine," I said.

"I'll try."

"Seriously, Grace."

"I know. I heard you the first time."

"You need to stop! I'll do anything. I'll go bowling in neon colors."

"Okay. I'll try."

"Grace!"

"Cassidy!" Grace shot back. "I'm. Scared."

"Oh, and throwing up makes you feel better? That is completely illogical!"

"Eating a lot all at once makes me feel really nice and full when I feel alone. It makes my stomach feel all warm." Grace seemed to physically shrink as she continued to speak. "It makes me feel less out of control. Then, when I want to feel like myself again – feel like fun, easy-going, overall-wearing Grace again – I throw it all up. And it's all gone, just like that. I can't make the Mean Girls go away. But I can make the food go away."

"That...that's horrible," I said quietly. I turned away from Grace, unable to keep my face under control.

"How is it any different from you staying up ridiculously late to finish all your work at once, and then when you don't get it done because you're too exhausted or brain dead, refusing to ever take a break, and still never getting any rest? And then when you do finally collapse because you're so exhausted, you sleep for, like, two whole days. Then you start over with the all work, no fun binge." Grace hurled the accusation at me, her voice twisted with cruelty and sadness. "It's the same horrible cycle."

"Those are not the same at *all*," I almost yelled.

"Yes they are! The only difference is mine is with food and yours is with sleep."

"Okay, stop," I said, suddenly feeling very tired. "Just stop!" I turned back to face her, aware that I was losing the battle with my tear ducts. "This could *kill* you!" I yelled.

Grace was silent for a long time. "I know."

"So you need to stop."

Then Grace started laughing. It was a happy laugh, and it sounded so beautiful that I wanted to slap her. "Wow," she said through her giggles, "that's such a great way to get me to stop, Cassidy."

"You know I'm bad at this," I said, the words serving as both an accusation and a plea. Grace was still laughing. "I never know what to say," I muttered.

"I know," she giggled. Then she took a deep breath. "I want to stop."

"Good." Then, before I knew it, "I'm worried about you."

"And I'm worried about you," Grace said as she reached out to hold my hand. I felt her pulse beneath her skin, jumping to let me know that she was alive.

Suddenly, I wanted to tell her all about John Brown. I wanted to tell her about how much he had cared about his family, and how he did kill people, but only because he felt his country had betrayed him. I wanted to explain how much this made me love history, but instinct told me that this was not the right time. So instead I said, "Okay." Grace tightened her grip on my hand. "I mean," I said with a smile, "thank you."

Grace smiled back, "You're welcome."

"I promise to respect my need to sleep," I said.

"And I promise to respect my need to eat."

"Good."

Grace leaned forward, and it was as if someone had injected life back into her. "You want to play a game?" she asked with sparkling eyes.

Honestly and truly, I was about to say yes, when I felt the tug of the unfinished paper in the bag slung over my shoulder. "Um…." I tried to think of an excuse, but Grace already knew.

"Oh my stars."

"Just this once."

"I can't believe you!"

"It's my final paper, Grace!"

"After the talk we just had...."

"But it's on refrigerator magnets, Grace! I did that for you."

Grace had turned away and crossed her arms, but I saw her begin to eye my bag. "Fine," she said eventually. "I'll let you finish your essay, *if* you read it to me first."

I backed up, my hand flying protectively to the bag. "What? Why?"

"Because I want to hear it!"

I was going to protest, when a realization struck me. "You're sure?" I said with a grin. "What about hating research? What about the world being better when everything is a mystery?"

Grace wore a guilty smile. "I don't know. Learning about refrigerator magnets doesn't sound too bad.

"You mean, you want to *learn*?"

Grace's smile drooped, and she scratched her head. "I, uh...."

My face stole Grace's signature smile. "Oh my God," I exclaimed. "Imagine! Grace Harper wanting to learn!"

"Just shut up and read me the paper, all right?"

"As you wish," I said through the smile now permanently engraved on my face. "Behind the Attraction of Refrigerator Magnets," I began, "by Cassidy Diamond."

chapter 29

I have spent more time reading textbooks than is good for me. For years, I have relied on them for almost every tidbit of information that is stored in my brain. Each and every question I have found worth contemplating has been answered by a textbook. But, as I sat in a hospital room and finished my final paper with the help of Grace Harper, something changed. I flipped through my many pages of notes on the physics of magnets while Grace hummed her classic tune and lamented her boredom, but I wasn't getting the answer I needed. My new question had become too big to ignore.

What do you do when you become too scared? I had asked Grace this question after she said that fear helps people accomplish things. But fear was such a slippery slope. Yes, fear might drive me to dutifully study for a test, but fear also drove Grace toward self-destruction. Fear of failing a test could lead to fear of being judged during a conversation, which in turn could lead to fear of facing the world. *So how do you fear one without fearing the other?*

I wondered if that was what had happened to Grace – if the fear of being judged had eventually become too much. But as she hummed away in her hospital bed, I realized I was too much of a coward to ask her. Maybe I would ask her another day, once I became better at those kinds of things.

I wondered if Likith felt scared, working every second of the day so that his parents wouldn't send him to India. I wondered if even Monroe was scared, worrying that one day no one would laugh at his goofy pick-up lines. Grace was certainly scared, trying her best to hold onto the qualities that set her apart from everyone else. And I was scared, battling the new fear that I was missing out on life, even though I had believed for years that the only way to get a life was to have none now.

These fears were real, but they weren't static. They weren't facts on a page that guaranteed a right answer. They could ebb and flow, and one day they could become too much to handle. *And what do you do then?*

By the time I finished my essay, Grace had long been asleep and visiting hours were over. I rode back with Mr. and Mrs. Harper in happy silence, though I knew I had a lot to worry about. Maybe I was too tired to worry. I was certainly tired.

In sum, the secret of refrigerator magnets' ability to grip the surface and not be dragged down by the force of gravity lies in the attraction between the atoms within the magnet and the surface of the refrigerator, which align and stick together. Whenever the pull of that attraction is greater than the force of gravity, the magnet stays where it is put on the refrigerator door. The attraction between the magnet and the surface weakens as the square of the distance between them grows. Thus for any particular magnet, we can compute the maximum thickness of the material – shopping lists, photos, etc. – it can hold on the refrigerator door without slipping. If the material exceeds that threshold, the magnet will plunge to the floor. It is this careful balance, this harmony, that must be established for refrigerator magnets to properly fulfill their purpose. The conclusion of my essay haunted me as I struggled to shut off my brain and settle down.

never trust a *happy* song

The next day, Likith and Monroe met us at the hospital. Monroe went in first to see Grace, leaving me alone with Likith.

"My mom should be getting into Palo Alto today," I said, staring down at my shoes as we leaned against the waiting room wall.

"Oh?"

"Yeah. She's surely going to try to move me to a different family right away."

"Are you going to let her?"

It took me several minutes to answer, and Likith let the time pass in silence. "I don't know," I said finally. Then, in a rush, "Actually, I don't think I am."

The corner of Likith's mouth shot up. "And what happens then?"

"All hell breaks loose, I guess," I said, and felt very happy.

Now Likith grinned. "I'm proud of you."

"Thanks."

"You're really smart," he said.

My eyes widened. "So are you!" I said, punching him on the shoulder.

"Nah, you're a different kind of smart," he said. "A better kind of smart."

I shook my head and looked down, my blush preventing a response. "Are you going to let your parents ship you to India?" I asked eventually.

I couldn't tell whether Likith was happy or sad, but his eyes twinkled in a way that I had come to define as uniquely his. "I don't know," he said, mimicking my previous inflections. I waited for the second part of his response, but it never came.

[*229*]

"You shouldn't," I said.

"Yeah, well," Likith said, waving his hand. "It's hard. *I* don't have a Grace to knock some sense into me. And I have literally two generations of adults relying on my ability to become a famous doctor."

I was still forming my response when Grace's parents came into view. Mr. Harper nodded at both of us, and Mrs. Harper smiled. "We're heading in to play a card game with Grace and Monroe," she said. "Care to join us?"

"Yeah, I should," I said, pushing myself off the wall. "I promised her a game."

"Sounds great. See you in there!" Mr. Harper said with a grin, his jovial attitude back in place now that his daughter was in stable condition.

I turned to Likith. "Come play with us."

"Nah."

"Come on! You always tell me I need to have some fun. Now I'm doing the same for you."

"And I appreciate that," Likith said with a laugh. I was about to drag him towards the hospital room when he jumped back. "But I've really got to go. I've got tutoring at 11." Likith gave me a smile that in the past would have convinced me he was fine.

"Well, okay," I said slowly. Likith smiled his goodbye, and was about to turn away when I reached out and hugged him. I hated hugs, and I'm pretty sure Likith did too, but it felt comforting in that moment. When I pulled back, I felt a little warmer. I was about to say something nice, when I noticed the evil glint in Likith's eye.

never trust a happy song

"Wow," he crooned. "I am so strongly attracted to you that scientists will have to explain the existence of a fifth fundamental force!"

"Eww, okay," I said, shoving him back. "The moment is over. You can go now!"

Likith doubled over with laughter before his merriment subsided and he left the waiting room. I rolled my eyes but then smiled, allowing myself to feel slightly ridiculous.

When I reached Grace's room, I was surprised to find that the game hadn't started yet. Grace was sitting cross-legged on her bed, while Monroe and her parents stood on the far side of the room. Mr. Harper still had his huge grin, and was clearly hiding something behind his back.

"Okay, Cassidy's here!" Monroe said, practically jumping up and down. "Can we give it to her now?"

"Okay, okay," Mr. Harper said. "We have a surprise for you, Grace."

Grace looked up at the four of us, clearly caught off guard. "Oh?"

"Yes," Mrs. Harper chimed in, stepping forward to kiss Grace on the head. "A gift for you, because we know that it's been a tough couple of months."

Grace's face lit up. "Oh, you don't have to–"

Monroe snatched the present from Mr. Harper's hands and shoved it into view. Grace squealed with joy, grabbing the gift from Monroe and hugging it to her chest. Only after I observed her joy did I realize what it was: a small magnetic board, complete with a set of word magnets.

"We know how much you love to make sentences out of the magnets on the refrigerator," Mr. Harper said, "so we thought you might like to be able to do that while you're here."

"Oh my stars," Grace managed, her smile so wide that it obstructed her words.

"Plus, I bought one for myself," Monroe added, dropping onto the bed next to Grace. "So now we can, like, communicate across the room through magnets. It will be totally cool. And Cassidy," he said, turning to me, "I got one for you, so that you could join in. You know, if you'd like to."

Now my smile was huge too. "Yeah," I said. "I'd love to." And I meant it.

"Balloons and a cake are on the way," Mrs. Harper said as she came forward to kiss her daughter on the head.

Grace opened and closed her mouth like a goldfish. "And this is all for me?"

"Of course," Mrs. Harper said, squeezing Grace's shoulders.

"But why?"

Mrs. Harper's smile widened. "We thought it might be nice to celebrate you."

Grace was dumbstruck, her eyes wide as saucers. She scanned the room, her gaze lingering on each of us for a long moment before moving on. After some time, Mr. and Mrs. Harper exchanged concerned looks. But it was clear to me that Grace was simply wrestling between feelings of joy and utter disbelief. And I understood.

never trust a *happy* song

It's crazy to think that people can appreciate your presence in their lives not because of what you've accomplished or what they've gotten out of knowing you, but just because you're present.

Monroe was the first to break the spell. He broke away from Grace and grabbed the deck of cards sitting on the side table, waving it like a weapon. "It is time," he declared.

"You don't have to be so serious about it," Grace giggled.

"Oh, yes I do. Go Fish is a serious matter. Now, Mr. Harper, Mrs. Harper, Cassidy," he said, turning to nod at each of us. "If you would, please join us on the bed."

Mr. and Mrs. Harper settled at the edge of the bed as Monroe began to deal the cards. I snickered at Monroe's pompous manner, which suggested that the dealing of cards was the most important thing he would do all day.

"What?" Monroe asked as he deftly completed the deal and looked up at me. "What do you find so amusing?"

"Oh, no reason," I said with a smile. "You're just funny."

I wanted to say something like that to all of them – something to let them know how much they mattered to me. But I didn't know how to phrase it, so instead I just smiled as Monroe passed everyone their cards, and our game began.

"Do you have any 3's?"

"No, go fish."

"Do you have any 5's, partner?"

"Dad, what are you doing?"

"Accessing my inner game-playing cowboy."

"Well, could you stop? It's embarrassing."

"I can't help it, honey. This game just puts me in that mindset."

"How? It's about *going fishing*."

"Or maybe it's about a boy's eternal quest to pick the perfect female fish from the sea."

"Shut up, Monroe."

"Make me."

"Kids…"

"Oh my stars!"

"Wait, how do you play this game?"

"Are you serious, Cassidy? We've played it before!"

"I probably blocked it out."

"Ugh. Just copy what I did."

"Um, okay. Monroe, do you have any 3's?"

"Yep! Here you go."

"What? When I asked you that, you told me to go fish!"

"I know."

"So?"

"So, I was lying."

"Are you *serious*?"

"Kids…"

"Yep."

"Oh my stars! I can't believe you! You're such a–"

And then Grace was yelling at Monroe, and Mr. Harper kept on talking like a cowboy, and Mrs. Harper was smiling widely, and amongst all this chaos I joined in, and next thing I knew our cards were flying through the air.

never trust a *happy* song

We must have looked crazy, really: three teenagers and two adults throwing playing cards at each other, yelling about fish and stars and who was going to have to clean up the mess. And then Grace stopped shouting and started laughing, and then we were all laughing. And that's all I really remember. In that moment, I wasn't thinking about any homework assignment I needed to complete, or grade I needed to improve, or test I needed to study for. I was just laughing. And it sounded really nice, all of us laughing together. It was the most beautiful sound I had ever heard.

thank you

Books are always an uphill battle to complete, but this one put up a extraordinary fight. Its existence owes much to the wonderful people who helped me along the way:

My mother. Without your advice, my books would never make it to final copy.

Gloria, for being my best first reader and loyal confidant. Thanks for listening to my crazy ramblings.

Olivia, for being my friend who keeps me sane.

All my dear friends at SAS. Keep holding on – we're almost to the end.

This book is about a subject that is very dear to me, so I am very thankful that I was able to form it into a story.

natalie bina loves to write, and is fascinated by how people react to the circumstances of their lives. She is also the author of *World of Chances, The High Road,* and *Vermilion Departure* – for all of which she owes a debt of gratitude to National Novel Writing Month. Natalie lives with her parents and two pet fish in Illinois, where she juggles her writing with being a senior in high school.

Made in the USA
Lexington, KY
27 March 2014